# Sisters Separated

Now how was Sarah going to help Christine? How could she have let her sister go off by herself like that? The next time Sarah kicked a rock from the side of the road, it was in anger, not self pity.

"You okay?" asked Hillard. He was looking at her with compassion, as if sensing that she was going through a rough time.

"I can't believe I just let her go off by herself. I just fell asleep in the back of the car and didn't wake up for hours. I just …" Sarah broke off with a fit of coughing. She had almost forgotten about her cold in her worry about Christine.

"*That* doesn't sound good. The cough, I mean, not the sleeping in the back of the car. Maybe that's where I should have left you. If you're sick, the cold air could make you worse."

Sarah rolled her eyes at him. "I'm fine. It's just a cold. My sister is the one we should be worrying about. She might be out here in the dark, all alone. And I don't see how we could possibly catch up with her, since she left hours ago."

Suddenly, instead of a rock, her foot connected with something metallic. It made a clunking noise as it hit a large rock off to the side of the road. Sarah's eyes opened wide as she gasped and bent down to retrieve the object. It was dented now, and the screen was broken in two places. But there was no mistaking what it was. It was the cell phone she had given to Christine before she had left the car.

# THUNDER

# AND

# BLOOD

## STACEY VOSS

Cover designed by Christina Wiens

Photograph of the Sleeping Giant
by Sonja Poperechny

This is a work of fiction. All of the characters and events portrayed in this book are fictitious, and any resemblance to real people or events is purely coincidental.

THUNDER AND BLOOD



First Edition, 2009

Published By:

Donner Publishing
424 York Street
Thunder Bay, ON P7A 7S2
CANADA



ISBN:        0981251609
EAN-13:      9780981251608

**www.thunderandblood.com**

Printed in the United States of America

To my husband Heiko, for helping me to realize my dreams.

To my daughter Paige, for being my best friend.

To Tina and Sonja for making my book beautiful.

To my mom, Pattie, and my friend, Leanne, for being such great proofreaders.

Finally, to those of you who enjoy my writing, thank you for reading.

In loving memory of my Grandmother,
Alice McCullough.


*Death a friend that alone can bring the peace his treasures
cannot purchase, and remove the pain his physicians cannot
cure.*

~Mortimer Collins~

# CHAPTER 1

Thirty-year-old Sarah Ingram slowly sipped her hot black coffee while gazing out the balcony window of her sister's sixth floor apartment. The weather outside looked deceptively warm for the middle of November and the slumbering stone form of the Sleeping Giant seemed to be reclining peacefully in the bay. The large peninsular land mass was a prominent landmark, best viewed from the Thunder Bay harbour front. It resembled a man, lying on his back, with his hands crossed over his chest. There were many First Nations legends about the large figure they called Nanibijou. Sarah's favourite was the one in which the spirit of the mighty Nanibijou called up an awe-inspiring storm to punish the white men for daring to steal silver from his sacred mine. After the storm, his people gazed across the bay in horror, seeing that their revered protector had been transformed to stone because of his magical exertion.

Sarah loved watching the sun rise over the Giant. She hadn't had many opportunities to just sit and watch the sun rise since she had married three years ago. She sighed resignedly and listened for the tell-tale sounds of her sister emerging from the shower. Last night they had made an impulsive decision to take a road trip to an expensive spa located just across the border in the United States. They had booked an overnight stay in the most extravagant room available and planned to take full advantage of the spa services. Christine insisted that they really deserved a nice, relaxing break from reality, and that Sarah's husband, Paul, deserved to foot the bill. Sarah had to agree that both ideas sounded good to her at this point.

Christine walked into the room, a big fluffy blue towel wrapped around her long, curly blond hair.

"Feeling recharged?" she asked, looking brightly, but carefully, at Sarah, almost as if she were afraid that her sister might fall apart at any second.

"I'm fine. Quit worrying about me. I'm just looking forward to a nice massage. Who knows, maybe I'll even get a manicure." Sarah was grateful for her sister's concern, but every time she saw that worried look on Christine's face it reminded her that she had good reason to be upset. She forced a smile to her face, trying to convince Christine that she was doing much better today than she had been the night before.

Last night, when they had called The Blue Cove Inn and Spa, the desk clerk must have thought that they were crazy, the way they were giggling when they had made their reservation. Or maybe he could tell that they were nearly falling-down drunk.

Three bottles of Rosé could do that to someone – or some-two as the case may be. The wine had been Christine's idea of how to cheer up her emotionally devastated sister. The silliness had helped to temporarily numb the pain, although it had returned all too quickly this morning.

Sarah did wish, however, that she had slept a bit more - it might have helped with the hangover she was currently experiencing. Her head was aching and she was too nauseated to even enjoy her morning coffee. The fact that she had a horrible cold didn't improve matters. However, her coffee cup, still warm in her hands, let off some nice aromatic steam that seemed to help a bit – as long as she didn't actually try to drink too much of it. The thought of the acidic coffee hitting her stomach made her insides cringe. Nevertheless, she breathed in the pungent scent, grateful for any wakening effects it might have. She still felt as if she was in a trance, but that wasn't solely from the wine. It was probably due more to the fact that her husband had, for all intents and purposes, destroyed her world yesterday. She pushed herself up out of the chair and thrust all negative thoughts back to the corner of her mind as she started to pack her things for the road trip.

An hour later, the two women were speeding down the road in Sarah's red 1992 Pontiac Grand Am, heading south. Sarah was at the wheel and singing soulfully along to the radio. The old Leonard Cohen version of "Everybody Knows" was playing, and it was the deep, dark kind of song that matched her current mood perfectly.

Despite the sunny start to the day, rain clouds were now suspended overhead and a thick fog had started to roll in. Thus far oblivious to the changing weather, the women chatted about inconsequential things as they sped down the lonely highway. Christine described some of the comedic antics of her grade three students in her class at CD Howe Elementary School. She'd been a teacher there for four years now, and she had yet to develop the cynicism that plagued so many of her colleagues. Christine still saw every child as her own personal project to mould and shape into a future citizen. She hadn't yet experienced enough disappointments to taint her sunny view of the world. Sarah hoped that she never would, but knew that the inevitability of some students falling through the cracks would eventually bring her sister's optimism down.

The fog was really rolling in now. The edges of the highway were barely visible to her straining eyes and Sarah could feel the adrenaline starting to flow as the driving became more and more hazardous. She slowed their speed to a crawl, afraid that oncoming cars wouldn't see her or that she would inadvertently cross the highway dividing line.

What normally was a vista of rolling hills, majestic forests, and lush farmland, was now obscured by a thick mantle of mist. The vapours were sliding over the hood and windshield of the car like blankets of silk and the combined effect was eerie.

Neither Sarah nor Christine was talking now. The conversation had just faded off as the driving became more perilous, almost as if their spoken words had been swallowed by the fog as well.

The road itself became rougher, and the small area of motorway that Sarah could see in front of the car changed suddenly from pavement to gravel.

"Well that's just great. Now I can't even tell if I'm on the right side of the road. Christine, watch for any houses or gas stations or … heck even just a light would be good."

Christine stared intently out of the passenger side window as they continued. Sarah was tempted to pull over, but she didn't know where the shoulders of the road began anymore and was afraid that if she just stopped the car they wouldn't be seen by any oncoming traffic until it was too late. To top it off, the gas gauge was now reading less than a quarter of a tank full. They had been planning to fill up with cheaper American gas at Ryden's Gas Bar, directly on the other side of the border, but it didn't seem as if they'd be reaching the border any time soon.

Suddenly Christine sat up straight.

"There's a light … over there … on my side, just ahead."

Sarah saw it now too, and pulled slowly and carefully off of the road and let the car coast to a stop in front of a small, rustic-looking house. She turned the engine off and they both just sat in the car, not saying anything for a few minutes.

"Should we go to the door?  Or should we just wait here until the fog passes?" asked Christine.

Sarah looked at her watch and saw that it was just after six in the evening. Her stomach was rumbling, reminding her that she hadn't eaten much that morning. She hadn't even tried to have lunch, given the upset nature of her post-drinking night stomach.

"I don't know if there's anyone home. It looks like there's a light on outside, so I guess it wouldn't hurt to knock on the door. This *is* awfully strange weather."

Sarah was just reaching down for the door handle when there was a knock on Christine's window. Both women jumped and gasped in surprise. They could see a big, man-shaped figure standing beside the car. Christine looked at Sarah for guidance, a look of apprehension bright in her eyes.

"Just roll it down a crack," Sarah said, her voice quivering just slightly.

Once the window was down, a pair of kindly blue eyes looked in at the two women.

"Well, hello there. Caught in the fog, were you? Not a very good night to be out. My name is Gerwin." The voice was unmistakably masculine, with a slight gravely tone, and a rough accent that Sarah found vaguely familiar but couldn't place. Both women visibly relaxed at the friendly tone of Gerwin's voice.

"Really strange weather today, huh? Started out all sunny and now this … fog." Christine peered through the open space of the window at Gerwin, and then impulsively rolled it all the way down before Sarah could protest.

Gerwin was a much older man, maybe seventy years old, with white hair and a wonderfully kind smile. His deep blue eyes were surrounded by the lines of age that Sarah liked to call 'crinkles' because of the way they bunched together when people smiled. His smile, so obviously genuine, reached beyond his eyes to every other part of his face. In fact, it seemed to almost reach right inside of Sarah and she finally felt herself start to relax.

"Would you girls like to come in?  My wife, Elke, was just making supper, and we would be happy to have you join us."

Gerwin's smile was infectious and Christine couldn't help but smile back. She looked over at Sarah, who nodded. Supper sounded great to their grumbling stomachs – and it would be nice to be inside and away from this almost unnatural fog. It actually reminded Sarah of a story from a Stephen King novel where monsters came out of the mist and killed everyone. She had read the short novel as a teenager and had suffered from nightmares about it for weeks.  This fog seemed to envelop her in dread and she just wanted to get out of it.

They got out of the car and walked towards the house. The house appeared to have been constructed using a very old-fashioned method, with logs instead of siding, a technique that Sarah really admired. She had always dreamed of getting away from city living and escaping to a more rustic way of life. She was startled, however, to notice that the light they had seen from the road was an old oil-lantern hanging from a brass hook by the front door. Gerwin noticed her reaction and smiled.

"Elke and I like the simple life. We don't put much stock in modern things, so we just keep everything old-fashioned around here"

Sarah looked over at Christine, who shrugged. It seemed strange, but she completely understood the sentiment. Modern life, with all of its technology, was certainly less physically demanding, but it added stresses that most people didn't realize.

Entering the house was like taking a step further back in time. There was no Ikea-style furniture here. Everything was made of wood and obviously hand-crafted. They entered directly into what appeared to be a combination dining and living room, with a lovely old-fashioned stone fireplace dominating the space. A roaring fire greeted them and Sarah finally began to feel that overwhelming feeling of trepidation that had been brought on by the fog melt away.

"Have a seat, and I'll tell Elke you'll be joining us." Gerwin spoke softly as he walked through a door into what must have been the kitchen.

Sarah plopped down on the couch. The blue hand-crafted cushions beneath her were surprisingly comfortable and the warmth of the fire helped to draw out not only the last anxious effects of the fog, but also the chill caused by the damp weather outside.

"This place is so cute!" declared Christine, "I love this. It must be so nice to live in such quiet solitude."

Sarah had to agree. The rough surroundings, instead of giving an uncomfortable feeling of primitivism, exuded warmth and calmness. It seemed like the perfect life for an elderly couple. She wondered what they had done before they moved out here and withdrew from 'civilization'.

Just then, Gerwin re-entered the room with a sweet-looking older woman that must have been Elke. In addition to the friendly crinkles next to her soft brown eyes, she also had a rosy bow-shaped mouth that smiled warmly at the two women.

"I'm so glad you're able to join us," she said brightly, "I've made too much food for just the two of us tonight and it will be a real relief to have some extra people help us to eat it. I would hate to have it go to waste."

Sarah only then noticed the delightful aroma that filled the house. It smelled like Elke had been slaving over the stove all day. She closed her eyes and inhaled slowly through her nose. There was definitely a roast of some sort cooking in the other room.

The two women sat down and waited at the big wooden table with Gerwin while Elke brought out the food. It was an enormous roast on a platter, surrounded by a wonderful assortment of carrots, potatoes, and turnips. It smelled absolutely heavenly to the two famished women.

"Is that beef?" asked Christine, curious because the roast smelled somewhat different from those that her and Sarah's mom had used to make for Sunday dinners.

"No, venison. We could never eat our cow. Bessie is like part of our family," replied Elke with a twinkle in her eye.

While Sarah was surprised to be eating deer meat, she found it to be a delicious change from her constant diet of beef and pork. Soon everyone was quiet as they got down to the business of eating.

After dinner, Elke brought out cups of aromatic herbal tea for everyone and they sat quietly by the fire, each lost in their own thoughts. Every so often, Gerwin would get up and look out the front window, almost as if he were expecting more visitors. Sarah was surprised that she had heard no other cars drive by. Usually, the road to the American border was pretty well-travelled, with many people driving across every day to either the Casino on the other side, or to the nearby cities of Duluth and Minneapolis for shopping or concerts. Maybe the dreary weather had scared everyone else off of the road as well.

Remembering her earlier musing about the prior professions of the couple, Sarah interrupted the silence.

"So, what did you two do before you moved out here?"

Gerwin and Elke exchanged wary glances. There was a momentary, somewhat awkward pause and Sarah was just starting to wish that she could take back the question when Gerwin finally answered.

"I was a … bus driver. Elke stayed home and took care of things around the house."

"Did you drive a school bus or a city bus?" Christine enquired, thinking about her students. Sarah could see how uncomfortable the couple seemed to be even thinking about the topic and tried to catch Christine's eye to get her to drop the subject, but Christine was leaning forward, waiting for Gerwin's answer.

Gerwin looked like he was trying to decide how to answer. Finally he just mumbled "a school bus" and took a quick sip of his tea.

Christine finally sensed that she had brought up a sensitive subject for him, although she didn't have any idea what could be so distressing about having driven a bus. She decided to drop the matter, rather than cause their generous hosts any further discomfort. Perhaps there had been an accident, or Gerwin had lost his license for some reason. They hadn't seen any other cars in front of the house when they had arrived; perhaps neither of the couple drove now.

After awhile, the awkwardness faded and Sarah began to yawn. It was getting late and both girls were exhausted, still not fully recovered from their late night girls' session the night before.

"Oh!" exclaimed Elke, looking distressed, almost as if she were experiencing some undeserved feelings of guilt for failing as a hostess, "You two have to stay the night. You can't go back out in this terrible weather. I'll show you to our guest room and you can get some rest. I'm sure the skies will be all cleared up by tomorrow morning."

Glancing out the window, she saw that the fog was still thick outside at the moment and Sarah had to admit that they wouldn't be going anywhere that night. The offer of a warm, dry bed was very attractive. Despite Gerwin's evasiveness about his job, the couple seemed very nice and completely harmless. Sarah looked over at Christine and saw that her sister looked exhausted as well.

"We'd love to stay. Thank you so much for rescuing us tonight," she smiled warmly at the couple, who smiled back.

Elke got up from the couch, took a candle from the fireplace mantle, lit it, and led them through the kitchen, and up a set of stairs leading from the back of the house. At the top, the girls saw that there was one door on each side of a small hallway.

"I hope you two won't mind sharing a bed," said Elke, apologetically.

"But I hope we're not putting you out of your own bed. We can sleep on the couch, or the floor," Sarah protested, thinking that the other door must be a bathroom.

"Oh no, that's our room right there," Elke said, pointing to the other door.

Sarah was a little confused.  She hadn't seen any other doors or rooms in the house that could have held a bathroom. Just thinking about it made her realize that her bladder was feeling quite full.

Elke seemed eager to leave them alone. "Well, goodnight girls," she said. "I'll have a nice breakfast waiting for you when you get up tomorrow morning. Sweet dreams." Elke handed Sarah the candle and hurried back downstairs before she had any chance to ask about the bathroom.

When Sarah and Christine entered the guest room, a feeling of utter relaxation enveloped them both like a warm blanket. The room was simply decorated, like the rest of the house, but the home-made quilt on the bed and the aroma of potpourri added the perfect touches to make it special. There was an oil-lamp on a dresser beside the bed, and the room was softly lit in no time.

"I'll just run downstairs and grab our overnight bags out of the car. I'll make sure to ask Gerwin and Elke about the bathroom while I'm down there," Sarah volunteered. Christine just nodded in silent agreement and flopped down on the bed, closing her weary eyes.

Sarah retrieved the candle and walked back down the stairs. She could hear Gerwin and Elke talking in muffled voices downstairs. She instinctively strained to hear what they were saying, but found that she couldn't understand a single word. It didn't even sound like they were speaking English. The conversation broke off abruptly when Sarah entered the room.

"I'm just running out to grab our bags from the car.  I'll be right back."

Gerwin and Elke shared another one of those mysterious looks as Sarah went out the door. Sarah was starting to wonder what they were being so secretive about, but felt bad about intruding on them.

Coming back into the house after grabbing the two backpacks from the trunk of the car she was greeted by more welcoming smiles from Gerwin and Elke. She figured she had just startled them by coming downstairs unexpectedly. It couldn't have been all that comfortable, after all, having two strangers intrude on them out of the fog without warning. She did have one more question to ask, however, before she could leave them in peace.

"Um, I was just wondering where the bathroom was?" Sarah asked, somewhat timidly.

"Oh, there's a chamber pot in the closet of your room. Just use that," said Elke, "I'll clean it out in the morning. Unless you want to go out back to the outhouse, that is."

Despite the simplicity of the house, Sarah could not hide her surprise at the lack of indoor plumbing. It made any questions she might have had about the behaviour of the couple when she had first come into the room vanish. Speechless, she nodded and went back upstairs to the guest room.

Christine was already asleep, snoring softly. Sarah went over to the closet, opened the door, and found the chamber pot there, just as Elke had said. She dragged it out into the room and looked at it speculatively. Part of her was happy that Christine was asleep and couldn't see her trying to squat down and use the chamber pot; the other part wished she was awake and could marvel with her at the utter lack of any twentieth-century technology in the house.

After doing her business she carefully pushed the chamber pot back into the closet, firmly closing the door and securing any unpleasant smells safely into the small space. She then slipped into a pair of pyjamas from her overnight bag and slid gratefully under the covers, expecting to immediately drift off to sleep. Unfortunately, despite being in a blissfully comfortable bed, Sarah just tossed and turned.

Her mind started out full of confusing thoughts about the couple downstairs, but it gradually moved on to angry thoughts about her husband.  He was a treacherous bastard! She unsuccessfully tried to keep her mind from replaying the events from Friday over and over in her head like a movie. She eventually succeeded, or so she thought, and finally slipped off into a fitful sleep.

*Sarah was getting out of her car in the driveway of the small house she and Paul shared on Oliver Road. She had come home from her job as a medical secretary after only an hour, because her bad cold had left her in no state to be having contact with patients. Working for doctors was a good thing — you never had to feel guilty about staying home, or going home, when you were sick. But the downside was that sometimes they also sent you home when you still felt good enough to work.*

*As she walked up the four steps to her front door, Sarah felt a sense of dread settle over her. She had been here before. She didn't want to do this. Her hand rested on the handle of the door, and although she tried to pull it away, her hand was stuck to it, as if it had been glued there.*

*Suddenly, Paul thrust open the door and glared out at her.*

*"What are you doing here?! You shouldn't be here! God you're such an ugly cow! You're worthless!! I'll suck every last little bit of happiness out of you if it's the last thing I ever do!!" He screamed at her, his face red with anger, his mouth twisted cruelly, and his eyes blazing.*

*He put his hands on her shoulders and pushed her backwards off the steps. Sarah fell backwards and kept falling.*

# Chapter 2

Sarah sat straight up in bed, gasping for air and trembling, tears in her eyes. Damn Paul! Her shoulders slumped and she was overwhelmed by feelings of defeat and worthlessness. It wasn't surprising that she was dreaming about Paul like that. She knew now that her deepest fears were true – she *was* too ugly and useless for him. She had always known it in her deepest heart. The fact that she wasn't as attractive as her younger sister had haunted her all her life.

She dragged herself out of bed, happy that there was no mirror in the room to show her the ugly truth. She wasn't thin like her sister. Her waist was thick in the middle and her legs weren't long and shapely. Sometimes she felt like she was some throwback from the Neanderthal Age. Her shoulders were too wide and her breasts too big. The only thing she liked about herself was her face – when it wasn't too fat. Her eyes were hazel, and when the light was right, they shone green. Her lashes were long and curled and she knew that other women were jealous that she never had to wear mascara. She wasn't fond of her nose, she had always felt that it was just a bit too big, and the way it turned up at the end was just a little too pig-like for her taste. Her mouth was nothing to look at. She always felt ridiculous wearing makeup and she found it impossible to find any shade of lipstick that didn't leave her feeling like a clown.

Sarah retrieved the clothes she had been wearing yesterday from a chair in the corner and put them on slowly. Her head ached and the bright morning sunlight streaming through the bedroom window was only making things worse. She had noticed when she awoke that Christine wasn't in the room and, listening carefully, she could hear her voice, and her cheerful laughter, coming from downstairs.

Sarah went downstairs. She could smell coffee and *that* distinctive aroma was something that could always get her moving in the morning, headache or not. It wasn't just her head that was aching – her whole body seemed to hurt this morning. This cold was really doing a number on her. Of course, she hadn't done her immune system any favours by drinking so copiously with Christine on Friday night, but it was something that had been necessary, dammit! It's not every day that you discover that your marriage is a sham.

Sarah pushed those negative thoughts back out of her mind as she entered the kitchen. Elke was bustling around the kitchen and the smells coming from the stovetop were heavenly to her growling stomach. Sarah was relieved to note that, despite her cold, she was starving.

Christine handed her a hot cup of black coffee as Sarah sat down at the table with her and Gerwin. She had a peculiar look on her face, which contrasted starkly with the cheerful laughter Sarah had just heard as she had been coming down the stairs.

"I think we should probably just head back to Thunder Bay today, Sarah. I doubt we have enough time today to really enjoy the spa, anyway." Christine looked anxious to leave.

Sarah looked at Christine carefully over her coffee mug. The coffee was wonderfully soothing to her sore throat, but she was distracted by concern about what could have spooked her sister.

"Sure. It looks like the weather has cleared up nicely." It was true – the sun was shining as brightly as ever and there wasn't any hint of the fog that had so enveloped everything the day before.

Christine glanced over at Gerwin. "I was just asking Gerwin how long the construction had been going on around here. He said that this road has always been gravel."

Sarah walked over to the window and just stared outside for a moment. She was positive that the road down to the border was paved all the way. Had they somehow turned off onto another road? That would explain the traffic, or lack thereof.

She turned to Gerwin, "Is this a side road off of the main highway to the border?"

He looked uncomfortable. "Might be. You should probably just drive straight back the way you came. I'm sure you'll find your way."

Sarah was sure he was lying, or at least not telling them about something. She just had no idea why on earth he would lie about the road. Before she could ask him about it, Elke came into the room, carrying a platter of eggs, bacon, and fried potatoes. Sarah ate quietly, thinking about all of the strange things she had noticed since they had met Gerwin and Elke. She silently debated with herself whether she should confront the couple, but decided against it, since they had provided such kind and undemanding hospitality. Once she had finished her breakfast she carried her plate into the kitchen and went upstairs to get her bag. Christine followed.

"Something weird is going on here," Christine whispered to Sarah.

"I know ... don't worry about it. We'll be out of here in a few minutes and then it's not our problem." They quickly tossed their few belongings back into their backpacks and, all packed and ready to go, the two women took deep breaths and went downstairs to say goodbye to their strange hosts. Elke had prepared sandwiches for them for the road.

"You didn't have to do that. I'm sure we'll be home before lunchtime," Sarah protested.

"Never you mind. You never know when you might get a bit of hunger in your belly."

As Sarah took the sandwiches from Elke, she suddenly felt herself enveloped in the woman's large embrace.

"Be safe," Elke whispered in her ear and then abruptly let her go and walked swiftly into the kitchen. Gerwin looked uncomfortable.

"Well, have a nice trip," he said, not looking them in the eye, "Watch out for strangers."

Sarah and Christine just looked at each other, mumbled their thanks for the hospitality and quickly walked outside to the car. The Grand Am looked the same as ever, if a bit more dusty than when they had left the city the day before. They tossed their overnight bags into the trunk and got in. Sarah noticed that the gas gauge was hovering just above the line reading E for empty.

"We'll have to stop at the first gas station we see."

As they drove off, in the same direction from which they had arrived the night before, Sarah looked back and saw Elke peeking out of the window with what looked like a worried expression on her face.

"What the heck was going on back there?" Sarah said out loud, more confused than ever.

The girls spent the next little while discussing the various things that had bothered them about the couple during their brief stay with them. Besides their seriously rustic living conditions, there was the fact that Gerwin and Elke had seemed so reluctant to discuss their past, and had seemed to be speaking in a different language the night before.

"Maybe they're here illegally from another country," suggested Christine with a shrug, "That would explain pretty much everything."

"Except for the fact that they seemed even weirder just as we were leaving," insisted Sarah.

She finally let out a slow sigh and decided to drop the subject. The odd couple was behind them now. It wasn't really any of their business if Gerwin and Elke were in the country illegally. What was starting to concern her now was the fact that this dirt road wasn't turning into a paved one and she didn't see anyplace where they could have turned off of the main highway by accident in the fog. She also hadn't seen any other houses since they left Gerwin and Elke's cottage twenty-five kilometres back. Given that it was only about a sixty-kilometre drive from Thunder Bay to the border in the first place, they had come quite a distance without passing any traffic, houses, or heck, even a moose!

Sarah didn't want to panic Christine, so she focussed on the road. To either side she saw only thick forest. In the distance she saw what might have been a big hill or a small mountain. It could have been Mount McKay, another one of Thunder Bay's landmarks. If so, they must be coming around the back side of it, because Thunder Bay would be visible by now if they were at the front. It looked vaguely familiar, but not enough so as to provide her with their current location.

It was at that moment that the car decided to sputter and stall. As the car rolled to a stop, Sarah swore under her breath. All she really wanted at that moment was to be back under some warm covers, nursing her cold – she would even have settled for the weirdness of Gerwin and Elke's house if she could just get some rest. This road trip idea had turned into a complete disaster.

Christine looked worriedly over at Sarah. Sarah's face was flushed, and not just from anger at the car. It was obvious to her that Sarah was at a breaking point – had been for the last few days, in fact. Somehow, luck was just not going their way at all. She put the back of her hand to Sarah's forehead.

"Jesus, Sarah, you're burning up. You shouldn't have been driving. You should've told me, I would've driven."

"Well, it's too late now. This car isn't going anywhere without some gas," Sarah snapped irritably.

"How about you just lay here in the car and rest for a bit? Grab the emergency blanket and curl up in the back seat. I'll take a walk and see if I can track someone down or maybe even find a gas station."

Sarah felt guilty about letting her little sister go off by herself, but had to agree that she wasn't in very good shape herself. She shrugged and let Christine lead her to the back seat and cover her with the emergency blanket. It wasn't the most comfortable bed, but at this point she wasn't in any position to complain. She just needed some rest. Sarah couldn't remember having felt this sick in a long time.

Just before Christine started off, Sarah had a thought.

"Wait a minute," she said, "I'm such a dumb-ass. My cell phone is in the glove compartment. We should be close enough to the city for a signal now. Try that first, before walking out on your own."

Christine retrieved the cell phone from the glove box and turned it on. Sarah had been keeping it off since Friday, just in case Paul had tried to call. There was no signal at all, not even a single bar. Christine tried it at various points around the car without any success. Finally, Sarah gave up and agreed to let Christine start walking down the road.

"Make sure you take the phone with you though. Try it every so often to see if you hit a good spot with a signal."

With that last piece of advice, Sarah lay across the back seat of the car, curled up under the blanket, and fell fast asleep.  She was snoring before Christine was even out of view of the car.

When Sarah awoke, she was disoriented. There was darkness all around her and she was shivering in the cold. It took her a few moments to realize that she was still lying in the back seat of her car.  It was pitch black outside and the temperature in the car had dropped substantially without the sun shining on it. She must have been asleep for hours!

Where was Christine?!  She should have been back by now!

Sarah jumped up and struggled her way out of the car. It was even colder outside and the brisk air did a quick job of waking her up the rest of the way. She could barely see anything by the light of the quarter moon, so she returned to the car and retrieved her flashlight from the glove compartment. That was one of the few good things her father had taught her – always have full emergency supplies in your car at all times. She shone the flashlight down the dark empty road. There was no sign of Christine, or anyone else for that matter. How could she have let her little sister go off by herself? They really had no idea where they were and there could be all sorts of dangers out there. Come to think of it, the prison was located right on the side of the same highway that led to the border.

'Good job Sarah, send your sister out to be raped or murdered!' she silently berated herself.

She called Christine's name out into the darkness for a few minutes before stopping herself, realizing that if there *were* any unsavoury characters out in the night, they'd be able to hear her too. She quickly got back into the car and locked all of the doors. She wrapped her blanket around herself tightly and thought carefully about what to do next. The car, in its current state, was pretty useless. It wouldn't be moving anywhere anytime soon without some gas.

Suddenly, she had an idea. She scrambled over the front seat and tried the radio. There was nothing but static. Now that *was* strange. Sarah knew for a fact that there was radio reception all the way from Thunder Bay to the border. There should still be something, even if they had turned off of the main road. Hmmm. The radio wasn't going to help. What would? In frustration, Sarah put her head into her hands and slumped forward. The horn beeped momentarily into the night.

Maybe someone would hear the horn. It couldn't hurt to try. Even if there were people lurking out there in the dark night, she had the doors locked. She beeped the horn again briefly – then again. Finally, she just laid into it and left it blasting into the darkness for several minutes, until she could hear the tone of the horn starting to change, becoming lower and slower, then she sat back into her seat and took a deep breath to stop herself from screaming out in frustration.

'Oh boy,' she thought, 'I should be careful not to kill the battery. With the luck I've had over the last few days, Christine would come back with gas and then we wouldn't even have the battery power to start the damn thing!'

Tears of frustration welled in her eyes. Why did everything have to be so hard lately? It seemed like her life had just turned to shit over the past week. It hadn't even been a week. It had all started on Friday morning as she arrived at work.


*Her boss had immediately seen that she was ill and had given her a stern warning about coming into work sick. Normally, Sarah would be glad to go home and sleep through the weekend to get rid of her cold, but she had used up all of her sick days and didn't have any vacation days left. That meant that she would have to take unpaid time off. That would certainly make her husband, Paul, unhappy.*

*Paul had been off work for the last six months, having been laid off from a local lumber mill. Finding another job for him hadn't been as easy as they had hoped. The job market in Thunder Bay had been suffering for the last decade, due to a lumber trade dispute that Canada had been in with the United States. Most of Thunder Bay's job market was dependant on raw material industries, so now there were too many unemployed people and not enough jobs for them.*

*Money had been seriously tight for them recently and it was beginning to take a toll on her marriage. Taking an unpaid day off of work was something she couldn't afford — financially or emotionally. Heading home, she dreaded the inevitable confrontation with Paul.*

*Sarah had pulled into the driveway and gone quietly into the house. These days it was Paul's habit to sleep late. If she woke him, he would be cranky and even less pleasant to deal with.*

*She had frozen as she entered the house. Through the door to the kitchen, she had been able to see a woman looking into her fridge. It was her neighbour, Judy.*

Sarah was startled out of her remembrances by a knock on the window beside her.

# Chapter 3

Sarah froze in her seat. Mentally kicking herself for her recklessness in honking the horn, her mind quickly switched to the problem of what to do now. She had no idea if this person was as kind as Gerwin and Elke had been (however strange they were) or if they had more ominous intentions.

Sitting absolutely still in the front seat of the car, Sarah was unsurprised to hear a male voice enquire, "Ma'am?"

She looked out of the window into the most penetrating pair of green eyes that she had ever seen. They were a deep emerald hue that seemed to look right into the deepest parts of her.

"I'm okay," she stammered, "No problem"

"Well," the man said slowly, "you were certainly making a lot of noise for someone with no problem."

Sarah listened very carefully, straining to detect any hint of malice in his voice.  She could hear none.  Generally, she trusted in her ability to judge people. She often knew, without being told, when someone, even a stranger, was upset or angry, even if they tried to hide it. In a situation like this, however, she couldn't afford to be wrong.

Still speaking through the closed window, trying to see more of the man, she said, "I was just trying to make some noise for my sister to hear. She should be right back."

The lie sounded obvious. Well, it wasn't a complete lie, she told herself, she *was* still hoping that her sister would return soon.

As the man gazed searchingly into the car, Sarah mentally kicked herself again.

'Way to go!' she berated herself, 'Now he knows you're alone!'

"Car break down?" the man asked.

Sarah noticed his relaxed way of speaking. He didn't *seem* like someone about to do violence. She would expect to hear more of a nervous pitch to his voice if he was. Then again, psychopaths, in particular, were known for their lack of emotion.

'Well,' she thought, 'if he meant to do me harm, the window isn't really going to stop him. There has to be rocks around that could break through pretty quickly.' Of course, if she had been thinking that clearly before she had started honking the horn, then she wouldn't have this problem at all.

She rolled the window down half way. The chilly November air swept into the car.

"Thanks for stopping. I'm sure my sister will be back soon," she said, trying both to give the impression that she was not alone and to give the man the opportunity to leave. At that point, something struck her as strange. She rolled the window down the rest of the way and leaned out. Looking around, she couldn't see another car in sight.

"How did you find me?" she asked, puzzled.

"Well, you were kind of hard to miss, with that horn blaring away," the man said, with a twinkle in his emerald eyes, "I'm Hillard, by the way."

"It's nice to meet you Hillard. I'm Sarah," she replied absently, then she looked him in the eyes. "But what I meant to ask was: how did you get here? I don't see a car."

He continued smiling at her, his eyes twinkling as if she had said something funny. "I was camping in the woods over that way." He motioned to the other side of the road. "I just walked over to see what all the ruckus was about."

That seemed like a plausible explanation to Sarah and she decided to ask, "Is this a road off of Highway 61 between Thunder Bay and the border? Christine and I – that's my sister – got stuck in the fog last night and I can't seem to figure out where we are."

An unreadable expression crossed Hillard's face as she spoke. If Sarah had to guess, she would have said that it was something between recognition and pity.

"Well, if you follow this road, you will eventually come to Thunder … Bay," Hillard paused hesitantly between the two words and Sarah experienced the same sense of suspicion and unease that she had experienced at the house of Gerwin and Elke.

Sarah didn't know what to do next. He was obviously hiding something. She knew that she needed help, but she didn't know if she could trust him. Getting out of the car could be dangerous.

"So, do you have a car out here?" she asked, thinking that maybe she could trust him just enough to give her a ride into town.

"Nooo," he said slowly, looking wary, "I've been hiking. I have a bit of wanderlust. I like to travel cross country on foot."

'So now he's homeless!  Great!' thought Sarah.

"I guess you haven't seen my sister around, have you?" she asked aloud.

"What does she look like?"

"She's three years younger than me. Prettier than I am. She has long curly blond hair and blue eyes. She's a bit taller than me too."

"Well, to be honest, I haven't seen anyone for a few days. I'd be happy to help you to look for her though. There are some rough types who travel on this road." Hillard looked genuinely concerned.

Sarah considered his offer for a moment. This guy was a complete stranger who had freely admitted that he was homeless. That didn't really fill her with confidence. On the other hand, she had to go out and look for her sister soon. Hillard looked like the kind of guy who would follow her anyway just to make sure she was okay.

That last thought made her pause. He *did* seem like the kind of guy who would watch out for her, and not cause her harm. She thought for a moment in silence before finally deciding to trust her instincts.

"Okay," she said, getting out of the car, "let me just grab our stuff from the trunk. She went that way. I think that's towards the city."

Hillard nodded, followed Sarah to the trunk, and took one of the backpacks from her. Sarah stuffed the emergency blanket into her backpack and after a moment's thought, added the first aid kit. She also grabbed the sandwiches that Elke had made for them earlier.

Outside of the car now, Sarah had the opportunity to get a better look at Hillard. His eyes were extraordinary, but the rest of him was not bad either. He had a really kind looking face and was a few inches taller than she was. He was wearing a worn leather jacket that buttoned in the front, dark pants, and had a large leather bag slung over his shoulder. All in all, he was a pretty good-looking guy.

They started down the road in silence. Sarah had her flashlight, but kept it off most of the time to save the batteries. Every so often, Sarah would steal a furtive glance over at Hillard. He seemed nice enough.

"So," she finally asked, "Where are you from originally?"

He smiled, almost wistfully. "Zwischenmeer."

"Never heard of it," she said. "It sounds foreign."

He just smiled and did not respond.

"What brings you here?" asked Sarah. The question seemed to give him pause. She watched as what looked like several emotions passed across his face.

Finally, he answered, "Family."

"Brothers and sisters?"

"More distant than that, although sometimes he feels closer."

That was definitely an enigmatic response. Then, Hillard looked over at her and asked, "Do you only have the one sister? Or are there more of you?" This last question he asked with a smile. The corners of his mouth crinkled and Sarah could see tiny laugh lines around his eyes.

"Just the two of us," she replied, "Our parents died when we were younger. My dad died of liver disease when I was only 16. I don't remember much about him except that he drank a lot and yelled at our mom. My mom died of breast cancer three years ago. Since then, it's just been me and Christine."

"So, you're close?"

"We're best friends, as well as sisters. She's always been there for me when I needed her – especially recently." Sarah's face darkened as she remembered the events of Friday morning.

Hillard looked at her quizzically but, before he could ask any more questions, Sarah changed the subject. "She's always been the pretty one though. Guys chase after her all the time. Not that she ever gives any of them a chance." Sarah smiled. "She says she's waiting for a guy with substance, whatever that means." Her smile turned wistful. "I never imagined that I would get married before she did."

"You're married?" If Sarah did not know better, she would have thought that Hillard looked disappointed.

"Was … is … not so much anymore," she replied lamely.

"Sounds complicated."

"Yeah, well, maybe Christine had the right idea when she waited."

"So what, exactly, did you mean when you said that Christine was the pretty one? That's the second time you've said that. I think you're very pretty." Hillard smiled at her and Sarah was surprised to feel her heart skip a beat at the unexpected compliment.

Sarah allowed her walking to take her to the side of the road, where she started kicking rocks self-consciously. She didn't answer for a moment. She never knew how to answer those kinds of questions. They always seemed so loaded and fake. Plus, the feelings left over from Friday morning were just too raw.

As if sensing that this was a delicate subject for her at the moment, Hillard fell silent, and Sarah became absorbed by her own thoughts again.

*After opening the door to her house, she had stopped in the entranceway, frozen in shock. Her neighbour, Judy, had been standing in her kitchen. Judy had been wearing Sarah's bathrobe. As she turned towards Sarah in surprise, the bathrobe fell open at the top, and Sarah could see that Judy wasn't wearing anything underneath the robe. Not surprisingly, the robe looked fantastic on the slender Judy — better than it had ever looked on Sarah.*

*Stunned, Sarah couldn't figure out what Judy was doing in her kitchen half-naked. Her mind just wasn't processing the visual information. Then Paul came out of the bedroom, wearing nothing but his white boxer shorts. He looked over to see what Judy was looking at and saw Sarah.*

*"What're you doing home? You're supposed to be at work!" he started shouting, accusingly, obviously trying to deflect the situation in her direction.*

*Sarah's first instinct was to defend herself and then she was overwhelmed with guilt at coming home without having earned any money for the day. Then an intense anger overwhelmed her. An icy cold feeling flooded through her skull and she couldn't even speak. She just stared at the two of them for a moment, her lips pressed tightly together, then she spun around, stormed outside and went back to her car. She pulled out of the driveway and began to drive around aimlessly, turning from street to street, unsure of where to go next. She had been driving around this for what felt like an immeasurable amount of time when she finally found herself in front of Christine's apartment building.*

*Christine had been home for lunch, but she had called in sick for the rest of the day after she saw the devastated look on Sarah's face. It had been Christine who had gone back to the house on Oliver Road to get Sarah's things. It had been Christine who had held her while she sobbed. And it had been Christine who had ordered Chinese take-out and opened the first bottle of wine. Her sister always seemed to know what to do to help.*

Now how was Sarah going to help Christine? How could she have let her sister go off by herself like that? The next time Sarah kicked a rock from the side of the road, it was in anger, not self pity.

"You okay?" asked Hillard. He was looking at her with compassion, as if sensing that she was going through a rough time.

"I can't believe I just let her go off by herself. I just fell asleep in the back of the car and didn't wake up for hours. I just ..." Sarah broke off with a fit of coughing. She had almost forgotten about her cold in her worry about Christine..

"*That* doesn't sound good. The cough, I mean, not the sleeping in the back of the car. Maybe that's where I should have left you. If you're sick, the cold air could make you worse."

Sarah rolled her eyes at him. "I'm fine. It's just a cold. My sister is the one we should be worrying about. She might be out here in the dark, all alone. And I don't see how we could possibly catch up with her, since she left hours ago."

Suddenly, instead of a rock, her foot connected with something metallic. It made a clunking noise as it hit a large rock off to the side of the road. Sarah's eyes opened wide as she gasped and bent down to retrieve the object. It was dented now, and the screen was broken in two places. But there was no mistaking what it was. It was the cell phone she had given to Christine before she had left the car.

# CHAPTER 4

The first thing that Christine was aware of was her aching head. Initially, she thought it was a hangover from drinking too much wine with Sarah the night before, but then she remembered the drive down to the border, the strange old couple, and the car running out of gas. The last thing she actually remembered clearly was walking down the road, shivering from the cold, then feeling a strange sense of calmness settle over her. She vaguely remembered being hit from behind.

Before opening her eyes, she listened to the sounds around her. There was water dripping some distance away, and someone breathing raggedly nearby. It sounded like the person was right beside her.

She cautiously opened her eyes and immediately became aware of the cold hard floor beneath her. She groaned a little as the world spun around her. It must have been a blow to the head that had knocked her unconscious.

"You're okay. You have a bump on your head, but it's not serious," said a deep male voice beside her. The man was wheezing a bit, as though he had a cold.

Christine sat up and looked at the man sitting beside her. He was dressed in what appeared to be old, but still serviceable, clothing. His dark hair was longish, not quite down to his shoulders, curly and tousled. His eyes were a deep chocolate brown and he was grinning at her like a little kid. He wasn't a little kid though, he appeared to be close to her age.

Her surroundings weren't so reassuring. Stone walls surrounded her, the perfect complement to the stone floor below and cold stone ceiling above. She was obviously in a prison of some sort. The problem was that she had no idea how she had arrived there in the first place.

The man sharing the cell with her must have sensed her confusion.

"They brought you in yesterday afternoon," he said, "My name is Gervis." He held out his hand to her for a moment. Then as if realizing that she was too stunned to take it, he lowered it to his side, self-consciously.

"Where am I?  And *who* brought me here?"

"Well, unfortunately, you're in Lord Radek's dungeon. His men brought you in yesterday."

"*Lord* Radek? What are we, in nineteenth century Britain?" Christine was getting upset.

Gervis looked confused. He didn't have time to explain, however, as there came from the hallway the sound of heavy boots approaching. The heavy wooden door swung inward into the cell with a creak.

"Girl! You come with us!" a rough, unshaven man, dressed in clothing much less serviceable than Gervis', demanded in a gruff and strangely accented voice.

Christine was torn between two bad choices. She could smell the pungent odour emanating from the two men from inside the cell, but the cell wasn't such a great place to be either. Her hesitation didn't impress her jailers at all. The man who had spoken first grabbed her roughly by the arm, then dragged her to her feet and out into the hall. Strangely, the two men left the door ajar behind her, leaving her with the suspicion that perhaps Gervis wasn't a prisoner after all. She heard him utter a weak "Good luck," after her before she was hauled up a steep set of stone stairs. From what she could see as she passed, the walls were all made of stone and damp with moisture. Green moss was prevalent in some places and she wrinkled her nose at the smell of old and decaying things.

After walking through several hallways, each gradually improving in condition, she was finally pushed into a room that was much more extravagant than what she had seen thus far. It had several colourful tapestries on the walls and the floor appeared to be made of marble. Two huge fireplaces lined either side of the room and the furniture, while old fashioned, was plush and obviously expensive. The room looked like it had been designed from a picture in a book about old castles.

Her eyes finally rested on the lone occupant of the room. He was tall, pale, and had long, greasy black hair. What made her breath catch in her throat was his eyes. They were an astonishingly vibrant shade of green. She had never seen anything like them. It was as if someone had plucked out his real eyes and inserted two perfect emeralds instead. They almost seemed to glow from within and she felt somewhat mesmerised by them.

"So . . . you are the new visitor from the fog, hmmmm?" His voice was low and rough, and would have been seductive had Christine not felt that there was something slightly unstable in his tone.

She nodded her head dumbly, wondering what the fog had to do with any of this, but she was too afraid to ask. The way he was staring at her made her feel decidedly uncomfortable. His intense green eyes seemed to be looking inside her and it was almost as if he were searching for something. Finally, he spoke.

"I am Lord Radek. You were brought here last night. We found you wandering alone on the road to Donner. I know you have come through the fog. That makes you a very special visitor."

"I've never heard of Donner. We were just outside of Thunder Bay when we ran out of gas." Christine was confused, and now more than a little afraid.

"I know things are a little strange for you right now. But you will soon become used to your new situation. You see, the fog travellers are a gift to me. *You* are a gift to me. Normally, I keep my *gifts* in the room in which you awoke, but," Lord Radek walked closer to Christine, grasped her chin steady in his icy fingertips and stared deeply into her eyes, "I think you deserve some nicer accommodations."

Christine wanted to tell him that she was no one's gift, but the words stuck in her throat. As she stared at him, he smiled reassuringly at her and she felt a seductive sense of relaxation overcome her. Her only thought was that he wasn't actually threatening her in any way. She looked at him curiously.

"How am I a gift?"

Lord Radek just continued to smile at her. The look in his eyes was almost searching and he appeared to be considering something. Finally, he nodded his head and spoke.

"I look forward to getting to know you better, Christine. If you wait here for a moment, I will arrange to have you brought to your new room."

He stepped just outside a different door on the left side of the room and Christine could hear him speaking softly to someone in the hall. She hoped it wasn't the dirty men who had brought her up from that cell. She didn't want them touching her anymore.

A slightly plump, kind-looking woman entered the room. She looked Christine over, almost in the same way someone would inspect a prized horse. She seemed to notice Christine's confusion and she smiled reassuringly at her. "Now, you just come with me. I'm Giselle and I'll help to make you comfortable," she said.

Christine followed her obediently. Passing Lord Radek in the hall, he stopped her and absently brushed a stray piece of hair off of her cheek with surprisingly gentle hands.

"You really are quite beautiful, Christine. Very special," he whispered in his seductive voice. He released her and stepped back into the room, leaving Christine with Giselle.

The hallway in which she now found herself was quite different from the ones through which she had been dragged following her awakening in the dungeons. These walls were clear of any moisture and they, like the extravagant room in which she had met Lord Radek, were covered in elegant tapestries. Giselle led Christine up a staircase at the end of the hall and then down another grand hallway in the upper level. Finally, they stopped in front of a thick wooden door that Giselle unlocked with a key. Christine entered a bedroom that was just as beautifully furnished as the fancy room downstairs. It was amazing. There was a huge four-post bed against one wall and a lovely dressing table opposite it. The only other furnishings were a large, ornate wardrobe and a fireplace.

Looking around her, thinking about how different this room was from the one in which she had awoken, Christine remembered the kind man from the dungeons.

"Who was the man who was with me when I woke up?" she asked Giselle timidly.

"Ahh, that must have been Gervis," Giselle smiled fondly. "He's Lord Radek's manservant. He just goes down there to make sure that new … guests are okay, especially if they have any injuries when they arrive. I'm sure you'll see him around the castle, but you mustn't speak to him. Gervis is a gentle soul and I wouldn't want to see him get into trouble with Lord Radek."

"Oh, but I would never … " Christine didn't even have time to finish before Giselle swept out of the room. There was a clicking noise after the door shut behind her, and Christine rushed over only to discover that it had been locked.

Something Giselle had said struck Christine as strange and she hurried over to the window and looked out. There, below her, was a grand courtyard. This really *was* a castle! Christine shook her head, as if to clear it. Maybe she had been hit harder than she had originally thought. How could she be in a castle? There were no castles within a thousand kilometres of Thunder Bay. Had she been transported to Europe while she was unconscious? The very idea was crazy. Her eyes rose to the horizon and she gasped at what she saw.

"Hello?" a familiar male voice came through the door, "are you alright in there?"

It sounded like the man that Giselle had identified as Gervis. Christine looked up from the bed where she had been sitting in stunned silence for the last half hour. She got up and ran swiftly over to the door.

"Gervis? Is that you?"

"Yes, are you okay?" Christine heard a note of concern in the familiar voice.

"What's happening, Gervis? Is this a dream? How hard did I hit my head?"

"Wait there, I'll come to you in a few minutes and explain everything."

She heard Gervis' footsteps echo back down the hallway and stared at the closed door. Was this some kind of dream or nightmare? She was trapped in a castle, held captive by some sort of medieval lord. The last thing she remembered before she had lost consciousness on the road was worrying that Sarah's cold was getting so much worse. It now appeared that Christine was the one in dire need of help.

She heard a noise coming from behind the wall opposite the window. There was a brief clicking sound and a section of the wall swung into her room, almost silently. There stood Gervis, grinning at her with a proud expression on his face.

Impulsively, Christine ran over and hugged him. Then she realized what she was doing and, chagrined, stepped back. Gervis' smile was bigger than ever.

"Are you okay?" Gervis touched her cheek gently, in the same place that Lord Radek had stroked it, but this time she felt a slight thrill rush through her body. Giselle was right, Gervis was a very gentle person. Having him there with her made her feel safer somehow.

"I'm confused, but okay I think. Unless I'm suffering from a concussion and a whole series of hallucinations. Then I am definitely *not* okay."

Gervis chuckled, "I'm afraid not. This is real. I know it's going to be hard to believe, but this is really happening. I'd try to explain everything to you, but I think it would just confuse you even more, and maybe even frighten you. I think you should just get used to things one step at a time."

"But Lord Radek ..."

"Don't worry about him for now. He's just left the castle for a few days. You'll be safe for now. That's one of the reasons I've risked coming to you this way. He's usually very aware of everything that goes on under his roof. And he would *not* approve of my visiting you. I don't know who would suffer more for it, me or you."

"Who *is* he?"

"He's the ruler in these parts. He manages the village and the surrounding areas. He's just left overnight for a visit to my parents. He's trying to find out if anyone else came through the fog last night."

Christine thought of Sarah, but still didn't trust Gervis completely, despite his apparent courage in coming to see her and her obvious attraction to him.

"You said that was *one* of the reasons you came here. What was the other?" Christine looked at Gervis, surprised to find herself almost flirting with him. He blushed.

"Well, you looked so pretty and vulnerable in the dungeons. I couldn't take my eyes off you when you were unconscious; I was afraid that you would disappear like a vision. We don't have many women come through the fog alone, let alone any who look … like you. I guess Lord Radek saw that you were different from the other fog visitors as well," Gervis looked chagrined, "he's never allowed anyone out of the dungeons before that I can remember."

Christine just stared at him intently, trying to read some sort of coherent explanation for her current situation out of his words. She felt as if she should feel flattered somehow, but she was lost in such a pool of confusion that she could make no sense of it at all.

There was a noise in the hall and Gervis nearly jumped out of his skin. He strode quickly to the opening in the wall and, as it shut behind him, Christine heard him whisper "I'll be back to see you tomorrow." Then she was alone again, if only for a moment.

The door to her room opened and Giselle marched in, carrying a covered tray. She set it down on the gorgeous redwood dressing table and motioned for Christine to sit down and eat. All business, she marched back out, without saying a word, the door locking behind her.

Christine sat down to eat and pondered her situation. First Lord Radek had mentioned the fog, and now Gervis had mentioned it too. They must be talking about that thick fog that she and Sarah had driven through the other night. It *had* been very strange, but it was hard to believe that it had the ability to transport her anywhere, which was what both men had seemed to be implying. She nibbled on a piece of dark bread as she tried to work out what was going on. She just couldn't wrap her mind around it.

After eating a few slices of bread with a deliciously strong-tasting white cheese, Christine felt herself overwhelmed with lethargy. She knew that she had been through quite a traumatic experience over the past twenty-four hours and she decided to lie down and get some rest, hoping against hopes that she would wake up in her own bed.


*His hands were on her, touching her, gently stroking first her arms and then her legs. It was so relaxing, so sensual. This was the most delicious dream that Christine had had in a very long time.*

*"Oh, meine Christine," murmured a deep gravely voice, "Lassen Sie mich Sie lieben."*

*Christine couldn't understand the words, but the feelings that went with them were full of sensuous warmth and love. She felt warm lips on her wrists, making a trail up her arm, over her shoulder to her neck. His kiss there was exquisite, better than any lovemaking she had ever experienced before. It was like a never ending peak of pleasure that just trailed on and on forever.*

When Christine opened her eyes she was very disoriented for a moment. The room was unfamiliar. She wasn't in her own bed like she had hoped she would be as she had been drifting off. She was still in the castle dream.

Dream? Did she dream while she slept? Christine felt a wave of warm embarrassment rush through her and she closed her eyes for a moment. What a dream! She thought it was no coincidence that she'd had a dream like that right after meeting Gervis. He wasn't the type of man she normally encountered – sleek, smart, ambitious and aggressive. Gervis was more the nice guy type, but more handsome than most. Most guys that she knew who were that good-looking were very full of themselves but there was something both shy and unassuming about Gervis. She smiled as she thought of him. At least there was *something* to smile about in this whole crazy situation. She couldn't wait to tell Sarah about him.

Sarah! Christine had totally forgotten about her sister, left feverish and sleeping in the back of their broken-down car. She had to get back to the car to find her. Of course, there was a locked door separating her from her freedom. Maybe Gervis could help with that. She was looking forward to seeing him again. Maybe she could convince him to leave with her.

Christine heard someone at the door and finally got out of bed. Giselle strode angrily into the room and slammed a tray down onto her dressing table. Christine noticed that the tray she had eaten from the night before was gone. Someone must have come in while she was asleep last night and taken it.

Giselle began to storm back out of the room, but she paused at the door for a moment, then spun around to face Christine. She had a look of utter fury on her face.

"I warned you to stay away from Gervis!" she spit at Christine, "It's all your fault that he's in trouble now! If you expected him to come visit you again you can just forget it!" Then she stormed out.

Shocked at the unexpected outburst, Sarah sat back down on the bed. Gervis was in trouble because of her! Somehow, someone must have found out about his visit to her yesterday evening. Numbly, she walked over to the dressing table and sat down. Nibbling on a piece of fruit, she thought carefully about her situation. From what Giselle had said, Gervis wasn't going to be able to help her get out of here. She was going to have to depend on herself. The question now was how she was supposed to do that.

She ate her breakfast, expecting it to help wake her up. Despite having slept so long the night before, she was still exhausted. After finishing her meal with a glass of milk, she walked over to the wall from which Gervis had emerged the night before.

It was solid stone. If she hadn't seen Gervis come out of there with her own eyes, she never would have believed that there was a door there at all. There didn't seem to be any way to open it from her side, no matter where or what she prodded or poked. Finally, her exhaustion overwhelmed her and she lay back down on the bed, thinking to examine the wall again more thoroughly after a short nap.

She was almost asleep when she heard a noise at the wall and the door swung open. She sat up with a smile, expecting her visitor to be Gervis. Her face froze when the figure stepped into the room. It was Lord Radek!

# CHAPTER 5

For a few seconds, Sarah just stood there, looking at the cell phone in her hand in silence. Finally, Hillard asked, "What's that?"

"My cell phone. Christine had it …"

As Sarah continued to stare at the cell phone, her brain tried to process why it had been laying on the side of the road, when she knew that Christine would have held onto it no matter what. After a moment, Hillard gently took the flashlight from her hand and began searching the ground around where the cell phone had lain. He wasn't gone long before he returned to her side. He didn't look happy about what he had found.

"Someone took her, didn't they?" Sarah asked quietly, a feeling of dread washing over her.

"Looks like it. Those rough types I talked about earlier, I would guess. But I have a feeling that I know where they took her. They wouldn't really hurt her, not yet. We should be able to get her back." "Shouldn't we call the police?"

That question seemed to give Hillard pause – he looked like he wanted to tell her something but was holding back. After a moment, he looked down at the phone in her hand and asked, "With what?"

Tears welled up in Sarah's eyes. She should never have let Christine go off on her own. Visions of Christine, clothing torn, blood on her face, began to flash through Sarah's mind. Her breath roughened and she began to cough again.

Hillard put his arms around her. "It'll be okay," he whispered reassuringly, "I'll help you find her."

Something about holding Sarah in his arms made Hillard smile, despite the seriousness of the situation. When he had first seen her, she had been so defiant and strong, and now she was full of gentle vulnerability that made him want to protect her. That was a new experience for him. Hillard generally tried to keep his distance from other people, whether physical or emotional. He felt like he was connecting with Sarah in a way that he hadn't connected with anyone in a very long time, and although part of him just wanted to enjoy the feelings that were rushing through him, it was something he couldn't afford right now, especially with someone like her.

He stepped back. "Come on. We'd best get moving. And I'm going to try to explain some things to you, although I'm not quite sure about the best way to go about it. There are some things happening around here that you're going to find hard to believe. When I first saw you there, in your car, I thought there might be some way I could ease you into this, but I don't think that's possible now."

Sarah was really confused now. She wasn't even sure how to respond to what Hillard had said, so she just decided not to.  She turned away from him and started walking down the road again, Hillard falling into step beside her after a moment. Sarah looked over at him, waiting for him to begin to tell her whatever it was he wanted to say, still having no idea how to respond to his strange declaration.

It was awhile before Hillard sighed, ran his fingers through his hair and said, "Okay, this is a lot harder than I thought it would be. I don't even know where to start."

He didn't continue. They walked on in silence for a few minutes, and then he sighed again. "Okay," he said slowly, "you know the fog you came through the other night?"

"Yes." Sarah was really curious as to where this was going now.

"Well, let me just give you a hypothetical situation. I want you to suspend all of your preconceptions and just listen to what I have to say with an open mind, okay?"

"Ohh kaaay." Sarah drew the word out slowly and had to work hard to stop herself from forming a wall of disbelief at the very suggestion of anything that might require her to keep an open mind. Things had been so strange for the past day or so that part of her wanted to close up at the very hint that Hillard might throw some more weirdness her way.

"Just imagine that the fog was a gate," he started, and now Sarah stopped walking for a moment and just stared at Hillard, searching his handsome face for any sign as to whether he actually believed what he was saying, or if he thought he was being funny. He continued, with the same serious look on his face, "a gate to another world just like yours, but somehow different. In this world, something happened differently in the past. This world developed in whole other ways from your own.  It's as if it were the same world up to a singular point in time where one person made a different decision from that which was made in your world, and at that point the two futures branched off in two different directions."

Sarah stopped and just looked at him for a minute. "You lost me at the point where you said that the fog was a gate. The rest of it sounds like some great Twilight Zone material though."

"Well, has anything seemed strange or out of the ordinary to you since you came out of the fog?"

Sarah thought about the road suddenly becoming gravel, without any visible sign of construction. She thought about Gerwin and Elke and their secret looks and lack of technology. Even Hillard himself was strange. To say that things were strange or out of the ordinary was somewhat of an understatement.

"Okay," she finally admitted, "Yes, some things have been a little . . . odd. But what *you're* talking about is impossible. I think, at the most, I must be having some kind of fever hallucination. It's also possible that you're some kind of lunatic, and I shouldn't be so trusting as to let you just lead me off into the dark like this."

Hillard sighed in frustration. He could see that he wasn't doing a very good job of explaining things to her. He didn't want to scare her off completely and have her decide that he wasn't a safe travelling companion. He decided to just let the matter drop for now and let things take their course.

"Well, fine, either *I'm* crazy or *you're* crazy. We can just leave it at that for now. I *can* promise you, however, that I won't let anything happen to you. I promise to keep you safe no matter what. How about we just don't worry too much about what I've been saying and just go and find your sister, okay?"

Sarah was only too happy to drop the bizarre subject and they continued walking down the deserted gravel road. The sun was starting to come up and Sarah could hear an entire symphony of birds beginning to sing in the trees around her. Despite the lovely surroundings, her cold was sapping a lot of her energy and she was feeling pretty exhausted from all of the walking.

Hillard looked over at her and saw how worn-out she looked.

"Do you want to stop for awhile?" he asked, a concerned look in his eyes.

"We need to get to Christine. Or, at the very least, we need to get to a town so we can tell the police what happened."

Hillard inwardly groaned. Sarah really didn't seem to understand that things were different now. There was no authority they could go to for help – the authority was the one who had her sister. However, the idea of resting, away from the hot sun, appealed to him.

"Do you have anything useful in these bags?" he asked.

"Just a change of clothes and some toiletries," she answered, realizing that if they were going to rest for awhile she really *didn't* have anything useful with her except for the emergency blanket.

"Well, I have a few things. They should do the job for now."

They walked off the road into the woods a bit and then walked parallel to the road for a short distance until they found a nice sheltered spot that looked suitable as a rest stop.

"What if there are wild animals?" Sarah asked nervously, looking around her, picturing a bear coming through the woods to kill them both.

"They tend to keep their distance from me," Hillard replied, with a hint of a smile. "Don't worry, I'll keep watch. You just get some rest. You won't be any help to your sister if you're really sick."

Sarah was too tired to do anything but watch as Hillard spread a thick fabric ground cloth on the mossy forest floor. She didn't have the strength to argue with him. When Hillard finished with the ground cloth, Sarah walked over to it, pulled the emergency blanket out of her bag, put the bag under her head as a pillow, and then lay down and tried to sleep. However, without the exertion of walking, her body temperature quickly dropped, a process that was sped up by the chill seeping up from the ground, passing all too easily through the cloth covering.

Hillard noticed Sarah's discomfort as she tried to wrap the blanket tighter and tighter around herself. Without saying a word, he strolled around the rest area, picking up twigs and small pieces of wood from the ground. Then he pulled some dried moss up and added that to the pile of kindling. He gathered some rocks, dug a shallow impression in the ground with the heel of his boot, and surrounded the hole with the rocks. Then he put the moss in the centre and started laying twigs around it in the shape of a tepee. This process took him all of ten minutes. Finally, he took a stone and his knife out of his bag and struck the stone sharply with the knife. Sparks flew from the knife, landed in the moss and, within minutes, there was a small fire going. Hillard dragged the ground cloth, Sarah and all, closer to the fire and wrapped the ground cloth up over both Sarah and her emergency blanket. Sarah was too tired to say a word. Then Hillard pulled another blanket out of his bag and covered her with that, too. Within minutes, Sarah was feeling warmer and finally able to sleep.

"But what about you?" Sarah asked sleepily, grateful to have someone take care of her, but feeling slightly guilty as well, thinking that Hillard was probably feeling the cold nearly as much as she had been.

"I'll just settle myself down over here and keep an eye on you," Hillard replied, walking over to a tree, sitting on the ground in front of it and reclining against it, as if it were the most comfortable chair in the world. "I like the chill of the autumn."

Sarah was too tired to argue, so she closed her eyes and gave in to the waves of sleep that were enveloping her. She was soon snoring softly.

Hillard just watched her. The tree he was leaning against was providing enough shade so that the heat of the sun was not bothering him too much. He would prefer to be in a complete shelter but, with Sarah with him, he hadn't been able to move fast enough the night before to make it to the cottage.

Sarah was an interesting woman. A bit stubborn for his taste, but he liked it in a way. She didn't just accept what she was told; she seemed to have an intelligent, questioning nature. She would be in for a heck of a shock when she finally accepted her situation. He just hoped that they reached her sister in time. Normally, fog travellers, once taken by Lord Radek, survived for about a month, sometimes even less. He reckoned that he and Sarah should be able to reach the castle in a day or two. He just wasn't sure how in the world they were going to get in.

Hillard closed his eyes for a bit, confident that the forest creatures would not want to come within a hundred feet of him. He smiled as he dozed.

# Chapter 6

Christine sat frozen in her bed, staring at the man who was walking confidently in through the passage in her wall. She had thought that Radek was out of the castle. That's what Gervis had told her yesterday.

Lord Radek didn't look as pleased with her today as he had yesterday. His hair still hung limply around his face, and there was a sardonic twist to his mouth.

"Expecting someone else?" he asked slyly, a hostile glint in his unusual green eyes.

Christine didn't know what to say. He obviously knew about Gervis' visit the day before. His words, combined with the comments made by Giselle earlier, made that all too obvious. She pulled the blankets up tightly around herself and just stared at him.

"Relax sweetling," he cooed dryly, "I know it was not your fault. Gervis is a bit soft in the head for girls sometimes.  I should have known that he could never resist you." He chuckled. "I have to say though, I did not know that he was aware of this passage. That was rather precocious of him."

Christine felt a wave of relief pass over her. He didn't sound too angry with Gervis either. Lord Radek reached down, grasped her chin between his rigid fingers and turned her face upward, so that she was looking into his intense, emerald eyes. A flash of fear shot through her, but it only lasted for a moment.

She suddenly felt an overwhelming longing to please Lord Radek sweep over her, overcoming the fright that she had initially felt at his touch. The last thing she wanted was for him to be angry with her. He was so fascinating and mysterious. She wanted to learn everything there was to know about him. She wanted … she wanted … his love. That's all she really wanted – to be worthy of Lord Radek's love. Some part of her knew that this was wrong, that these feelings were not her own, but she was unable to resist the strong urge to please the man in front of her.

Christine found herself smiling radiantly at Lord Radek and he smiled back.

"Oh, how lovely. Sweetling, you have the loveliest smile. I wish I could see it more often."

Christine's smile widened. She was so happy he was there! She jumped up from the bed and threw her arms around Lord Radek, burrowing her face in his shoulder.

"Please don't be angry. I don't want you to ever be angry with me," she begged.

Lord Radek chuckled. He took Christine's hand and led her back to the bed. He lay her down on her back, and began gently running his fingers up and down her legs and her arms very sensuously, lifting the hem of her nightgown and sliding his fingers underneath.

"You are so very lovely, Christine," he murmured, "I could never be angry with you."

Christine's mind drifted back to her wonderful dream. She realized now that it hadn't been a dream at all. It had been Lord Radek. His wonderful kisses. His sensuous touch. She felt like she would never need another man as long as she had Lord Radek. Any romantic thoughts of Gervis had evaporated from her mind.

"That is right, my sweet. You will never need anyone else. Until the day you die, I will be your everything."

When Christine opened her eyes, she could tell that it was late afternoon by the change in the angle of the sun's rays through her window. As she looked around her room, wondering if Radek was still there, she found Giselle looking down at her with a look of disgust on her face.

"Are you going to stay in bed all day? You've only been here one day. I hope you don't think I'm here to wait on you hand and foot." With that comment, Giselle stormed out of the room, carrying the morning dishes with her. Christine took note of the sound of her locking the door behind her.

She was in bed. How had she gotten there? She remembered having breakfast, then looking for some way to access the passageway. Then she had decided to take a nap. But ... something else.

It all came flooding back and Christine felt the colour rush to her face. Lord Radek had been there! Her mouth twisted in disgust as she remembered her behaviour towards him. Had she really fawned over him like that? What the hell had come over her? Maybe she really did have a concussion! The warmth from her face spread as she remembered what she had let … no … encouraged … Lord Radek to do to her. It could have been worse – she didn't remember actually having sex with him – but what she *did* remember was bad enough. She felt dirty and violated and yearned for some way to wash herself to somehow get clean again.

She had to get out of there, that's all there was to it. This place was doing strange things to her mind. Christine sat up in bed, then lay immediately back down as a wave of dizziness enveloped her. Concussion seemed to become a more likely explanation by the minute. And she was so very tired. She knew that Giselle was right, and she shouldn't spend all day in bed, but she didn't see that she had anything else to do in her luxurious prison. A bit more rest couldn't hurt. When she was more awake she could think up an escape plan.

Christine closed her eyes, and she was fast asleep in seconds.

When Sarah awoke, the light was already growing dim. She sat up quickly, which set off a fit of coughing. Hillard came quickly over and handed her a cup of tea in a tin cup.

When the fit finally passed, Sarah sipped the tea. It wasn't black tea, it smelled strongly of ginger. It had the combined effect of warming her chilled bones and soothing her raw throat, which felt like it was lined with razor blades. Her cold was definitely developing into something worse.

"I'm sorry I don't have anything for you to eat," Hillard apologized, "but we should be at the cabin of a friend of mine later on tonight. She'll have something I'm sure."

Sarah was surprised at the pang of jealousy that shot through her when she heard Hillard use the pronoun 'she' for his friend. His girlfriend maybe? Why should she care? He was just some homeless guy who was helping her to find her sister. She reached into her bag and grabbed the sandwiches that Elke had prepared for her and Christine the day before and handed one to Hillard. Sarah was too hungry to worry about spoilage – the sandwiches tasted great, although it was extremely painful to swallow. She used the tea to wash the sandwich down more gently. Once she had finished, Hillard handed the other sandwich back to her, uneaten, insisting that he wasn't hungry and that she needed the strength to travel and fight off her illness. She took it gratefully and soon there was nothing left but crumbs.

She felt ashamed of her jealous thoughts when she realized that Hillard had kept the fire going for her all day and had left her with all of the blankets as she slept. The crisp November air was chilly and she knew that he must have been cold. So what if he *did* have a girlfriend? She shouldn't be surprised. He was attractive, caring, and charming. Besides, what right did she have to be jealous? It wasn't like he would ever be interested in someone like her.

"Are you sure you're okay to travel?" he asked, as he looked her over with concern in his eyes. She didn't look at all well. Her face was flushed with fever and her breathing was ragged. He needed to get her to some real shelter soon, or she would become too sick to walk. He was developing a  need for some real shelter as well. He couldn't spend another entire day out in the sunlight without feeding.

He considered trying to heal her, but suspected that she wouldn't react well. In fact, if she had any idea of his true nature it was likely that she would panic and flee. Then she would be worse off than she was now.

"I'm fine," she insisted, crossly. She wasn't really angry at him for being concerned. She was more irritated with herself for her feelings of jealousy.

Hillard began folding the blankets and putting them back into his bag while Sarah finished her tea. He handed her the folded emergency blanket. Silently, she put it back into her bag. She told herself that she was being silly. She really needed to pull herself together so that she could find and rescue Christine.

That last thought got her moving. She handed the empty cup to Hillard and started walking towards the road, before Hillard had a chance to put the cup in his bag.  She had spent the entire day sleeping! Who knew what was happening to Christine while she was lying around.

They walked down the road in silence for awhile. Sarah was concentrating on breathing – her lungs hurt and she was pretty sure that her fever was still high. For some reason she started thinking about the outrageous hypothesis that Hillard had thrown at her earlier. It was an interesting idea, that the fog was a gate, and she was in a parallel universe. She smiled. It sounded like something that would be a good plot for a fantasy novel.

As she walked, she looked around, trying to identify any familiar landmarks. The small range of large hills that she had thought earlier were part of Mount McKay *was* similar to what she would expect if she were heading into Thunder Bay. The only problem was the lack of houses along the way and the absence of the two major ski facilities – Loch Lomond and Big Thunder. Normally, the paths for skiers, cut through the thickly forested hillside, were obvious. There was no sign of them here.

About an hour later, they came to a broad river. There was a wide wooden bridge spanning the water. Something about the river seemed familiar, but Sarah pushed all of those kinds of thoughts away. She continued to insist to herself that they were on some road that possibly ran parallel to the highway. She and Christine must have just somehow turned off the highway in the fog. It wasn't *that* unlikely. She hadn't been able to see five feet ahead of her at the time, let alone the sides of the road. She could easily imagine that they had gotten off-track. Any other explanation was just impossible.

Hillard silently watched his travelling companion. She looked really rough. Her cold was obviously developing into some sort of secondary infection and he hoped that she would make it to the cottage. He knew that he could carry her, if necessary, but while carrying a woman and three bags was not something that would tax him or his abilities, Sarah's reaction to such a feat was not an idea that appealed to him.

The night grew darker and darker and there were clouds covering the moon. Soon, Sarah was having a hard time even seeing a few feet in front of her. It reminded her of driving through the fog. She pushed that thought out of her mind again, not wanting to think about it, or the implications of what Hillard had been trying to tell her earlier.

After almost tripping over some loose stones on the road that she didn't see because of the darkness, Sarah reached out and grabbed Hillard's hand. He didn't seem to have any trouble at all seeing in the dark. She considered using her flashlight, but didn't want to run out of batteries and thought that they might need it if the night grew any darker.

Hillard tried to ignore the feeling of Sarah's warm hand in his. It was actually quite hot – her fever must be really high. Part of him felt so protective of her, the other part wanted to run away from the attraction he felt towards her. He couldn't afford to get involved with someone as innocent as she was. He had too many obligations towards Adalaide.

Sarah was starting to feel a little dizzy and was happy to have Hillard's steady hand in her own. They reached a crossroad and Hillard led her off to the right. She still had no idea where they were, but decided to trust that Hillard was the nice guy he appeared to be. He had taken very good care of her at their last stop. If he had less than innocent intentions, he could have made his move back then. He'd had her at his mercy while she had been sleeping. He essentially had her at his mercy now, too, while she couldn't see and didn't have any idea where she was. But for some reason she felt safe with Hillard.

"How long until we get to the cottage?" she asked, after what seemed like an eternity since they had left their resting place.

"We should be there within the hour," he said. "We'll reach the lake soon and then we just follow the shore to Adelaide's cabin."

'Adalaide,' Sarah thought, 'So that's what her name is.' Jealousy reared its ugly head again and Sarah pictured what Adalaide might look like. She was probably a tall, leggy blond, with big breasts and a tiny waist. She most likely had blue eyes and the face of an angel. Unable to help herself, Sarah asked, "Is she pretty?"

Hillard thought for a moment before answering. "She's beautiful. She's very full of life and, although she doesn't always realize it, she has a really good heart." He looked like he was lost in thought after he answered and Sarah didn't want to interrupt him by asking any more questions. His tone had answered her next question anyway – it was obvious that he had some very deep feelings for this woman.

Sarah didn't know why she'd even bothered asking. She'd just met this guy. Besides, she was still married to Paul, the asshole that he was. She just focussed on walking, watching the ground in front of her. It felt as though they had been walking for hours, and perhaps they had – Sarah's sense of time was as muddled as her stuffy head. Nevertheless, they must be getting close to the city by now.

She knew she was right when she began to hear the cries of seagulls in the distance. They must be in close proximity to the lake. The sun was starting to come up and she was relieved to finally be able to see what was under her feet and directly in front of her.

The lake, of course, was Lake Superior, the largest fresh water lake in the world. Whenever Sarah travelled away from Thunder Bay, it was always the lake that she missed most, much in the same way she imagined people who lived next to the ocean felt about their 'big water.' It was a majestic sight to see, the water stretching so far out into the distance that you couldn't see the other side. It really did look like an ocean, if you didn't know better, and couldn't tell the difference in smell between fresh water and salt. It was just a few days ago that Sarah had been sitting in Christine's apartment, sipping her coffee and gazing out, over the lake, and admiring her old friend the Sleeping Giant.

The road Sarah and Hillard were on came to an end, branching out into two paths perpendicular to the original road. Sarah looked at Hillard for any indication of which path to take.

Hillard had paused, an idea tickling at the edges of his mind. Finally he nodded, as if he had made a big decision, tightened his grip on Sarah's hand and said, "Follow me. I think there's something you need to see." Still holding her hand, he led her straight ahead, into the woods. They tromped through the wild woods, no open path available to them, thickets scratching at them, climbing over the big pieces of deadwood that blocked their way. Finally they emerged onto a flat expanse of rock which Sarah recognised immediately as part of the Canadian Shield. It led into the unmistakable waters of Lake Superior. There, far out in the bay, was her familiar friend the Sleeping Giant. The sun was rising behind it and it was as beautiful as ever.

Sarah just stared at it for a moment until she realized that something wasn't right about her view. The vista she had of the

Giant was one that she would have had if she were standing in Marina Park. Normally, the Giant looked different, depending on where you were looking at it from – that's how she knew that she should have been standing at the Marina. From the back, and from the top of Mount McKay, the Giant almost looked like a woman, with rock protruding where two breasts might be. From Marina Park, the protrusion looked more like an Adam's apple. As she stared out into the bay, she realized that the discomfort she felt was related to the fact that something else was missing from her view – there was no breakwater and no lighthouse – two items that would be visible at any point along the western shore near the city.

She turned around and looked behind her, trying to spot the city that she knew should be there. There was forest – pine trees and birch trees - in abundance. There was a hill, where she knew Port Arthur sloped upward to Hillcrest Park and there, at the top of the hill, where the doctor's houses normally stood, looking out at the best view in the city, was a castle – a real, stone castle. Sarah turned back around and looked at the Giant. There were no castles anywhere near Thunder Bay, she knew that. She turned back and looked at the castle again, then turned back to the water. Sarah repeated that action several times until, finally, the spinning didn't stop and she was overwhelmed by dizziness. Darkness closed over the edges of her vision, and her last thought before fainting was 'Oh my God, he was right. The fog *was* a gate.'

# Chapter 7

Hillard had been watching Sarah's reaction at seeing the land mass stretching out across the lake. He watched her turn back and forth from the lake to the castle on the hill and back again with pity. He had been born in this world, so he'd never experienced what she was feeling first hand, but he'd seen a similar reaction several times in others and it never became any easier to watch.

As Sarah slumped to the ground, he rushed forward to catch her but, despite his more-than-human speed, he was too late. He knelt beside her and gazed down at her pale face. Her light brown shoulder-length hair was fanned around her face like a halo and she looked achingly beautiful. The feverish flush only added to her loveliness. He gently stroked her cheek and his finger trailed down the surface of her face, and along the side of her throat. There he paused.

He mustn't even think about it. It had been days since he had fed, but they would be at Adalaide's cottage soon enough. With a sigh, he reached his right hand behind her shoulders and took hold behind her knees with the left. Rising, he could feel the heat from her fever through her clothing, and he swore softly. She was very ill.

On a positive note, however, he could now move at his full speed, and they would be at Adalaide's cottage in mere moments. Carefully, he picked his way back through the forest to the point where the road met the path. Neither branch nor twig touched Sarah as he passed.

Once he reached the path, however, he sped up, moving at a speed that would be unnaturally fast for a human. He was not human, however, he was something more. He had been human once, but that was more than fifty years ago.

When Christine awoke, it was dark. She felt slow and groggy. Trying to wake up fully, she felt like she was swimming up toward the surface of a warm deep pool. She wondered if she had been drugged. She tried to think back and determine whether every time she'd had something to eat she'd felt the same irresistible urge to sleep. It would have been an easy explanation, but Christine realized that she had felt constantly tired since she had first awoken in the castle. It could have something to do with the knock she had taken on the head.

After a few minutes of deep breathing, she was finally awake enough to sit up. She felt weak and feverish and she wondered if she had caught Sarah's cold. That could also explain the sleepiness. It didn't have to be something as nefarious as drugging or as medically worrisome as a concussion.

Getting out of bed, she sighed as her feet came to rest on the cold floor. She slowly walked over to the dressing table and sat down. There was a basin of cool water there and she was happy for the opportunity to finally wash herself, if even in such a limited fashion. What she wouldn't give for a nice hot bath right now. The chilly water, however, felt cool and refreshing on her tired sweaty face. The water finally washed away the remnants of sleep and she got up again and walked over to her bedroom window.

She hadn't looked outside again since she had first arrived in her room. Now, she gazed out and saw, in the light of the half moon, the Sleeping Giant reclining across the bay.

Christine wasn't sure exactly what was going on, but she knew that she hadn't been transported to some European castle while she was unconscious. The view she saw now was very nearly the same as the one she saw every day from the kitchen in her apartment in Waverly Towers. Now that her head was clearing, she tried to understand how such a situation could be possible. She thought back to Saturday afternoon, which was the last time that she had known things were normal. She and Sarah had left her apartment at around two in the afternoon, driving south towards the border to the United States. It had started out sunny and they had been chatting and laughing about their hangovers and their over-indulgences from the night before. Then they had hit bad weather. That was where things had started to become strange – in the fog. Everything had been weird since then.

Gervis and Elke had been nice enough. Their house had been remarkably quaint, but it wasn't as if Christine had never heard of people who pulled away from today's overly technologically-obsessed society. In fact, she'd even had a friend who had grown up in a rural area located just outside of Thunder Bay, in a small house with no running water and an outhouse as the only bathroom. So Christine hadn't been overly concerned about the simplicity of Gerwin and Elke's living conditions.

However, in retrospect, when combined with the sudden transformation of the highway from pavement to gravel, the complete lack of houses or any other signs of civilization along the road, and now finding herself in a castle located in the middle of what should have been Thunder Bay, Christine was starting to realise that something was seriously amiss.

"Toto, I don't think we're in Kansas anymore;" she joked aloud to herself, and then became more solemn as she thought about her sister. She wondered if Sarah was still waiting for her in the car or if she had left it and was now walking down the empty road, not understanding what had happened to them or where they were. Perhaps she, too, had been captured and was now trapped in the castle wondering where Christine was.

With that thought, she released the latch on the window and let the glass swing into the room. Her intent had been to lean out the window and see what she could of the castle, but she stopped when she saw the thick metal bars blocking the way.

"Christine, you're seriously trapped here," she said aloud, using the calmness of her spoken voice to still her inner self and prevent the scream that was bubbling up inside her from coming to fruition.

She had no way to escape. She was completely trapped in this room, in this castle, at the mercy of a crazy man. Her mind started working methodically, her eyes searching the dim room for some weakness, some hope of escape.

Systematically, she began at the window and began to carefully inspect her room. Her walls, like the walls in the room downstairs, were covered in tapestries, the purpose of which seemed to be both as decoration and as insulation against the cold seeping in from outside through the stone walls. The room was sparsely furnished, with only the bed, the dressing table, and a wardrobe lining the walls, leaving an enormous empty space in the middle of the room, which was covered by a lavish oriental-style rug.

She went over to the dressing table, inspecting it as if seeing it for the very first time. It was made of heavy redwood, expertly crafted, the surface gleaming in the dim light of the moon. There was an oval mirror at the back, with artistic carvings of nude women surrounding the glass. It seemed like an odd motif for a ladies' dressing table.

Christine went back to the tapestry lining the wall beside the window. She inspected it more cautiously, taking careful note of the design and decorative aspect of the piece. The picture was simple, but disturbing. It depicted a dinner scene in a large dining room. There were twelve people seated at the table, with one man at the head. Strangely, he had numerous wine glasses in front of him, all empty except for some residue of what looked like red wine. That's what Christine assumed it was until her gaze travelled to a man on the far end of the table. He held a blade to his wrist, and blood was dropping down the blade and into a wine glass.

Christine stared at the tapestry scene in fascinated horror. Was it some sort of religious blood sacrifice? It was a very strange choice of art to hang in a bedroom. Of course, nothing here had seemed normal since she and Sarah had come through the fog.

There was a noise at the door and Giselle entered. She looked at Christine for a moment, then finally spoke, a distrustful look on her face.

"The master would like you to join him for dinner," she said. There was an almost angry tone to her voice.

Christine saw this as an opportunity to get out of the beautiful but stifling room and see more of the castle. If she was going to escape, she had to at least have some idea of where she was. When she was first brought up to this room, she hadn't thought to inspect her surroundings. All she remembered was a blur of grey stone walls and cold stone floors. She couldn't remember in which direction they had travelled or even what exact floor she was on. In effect, she was lost in the castle with no idea of how to get out.

Another thought crossed her mind. Perhaps she would see Gervis when she was out of her room, walking in the castle. Maybe he could still help her to escape. He had suggested something like that when he had come to her the first night. Thinking about it more, she stopped that thought before she could get her hopes up. She couldn't risk getting herself or Gervis in trouble, and Lord Radek had made it all too clear that they were not to see each other. Christine finally decided to just pretend to ignore Gervis if she saw him, only giving him some sign of recognition and friendliness if she had a moment when no one else was looking.

Giselle was still staring at her impatiently. Christine had the distinct impression that the woman didn't like her or approve of her for some reason, aside from her responsibility in getting Gervis in trouble.

"Oh, of course I'll have dinner with him. But I don't have any clothes except for this nightgown." She had been wearing the nightgown when she had first awoken in the dungeon. By this time it was dirty and smelled of old sweat. Christine wondered who had undressed her when she had first arrived at the castle – Gervis, or one of the guards. She blushed, but hoped that it had been Gervis. The thought of one of those smelly, unkempt guards touching her naked body revolted her.

Giselle snorted and walked over to the wardrobe. Throwing the doors open wide, she exposed a plethora of silks and satins in a wide variety of colours. Christine gasped. She had never seen such a huge assortment of beautiful clothing in her entire life.

"But will they fit?" Christine asked, incredulous that such an extravagant wardrobe could be available to her.

"Of course they will. Master picked them out especially for you," muttered Giselle.

Christine had no idea how Lord Radek could know her size, let alone when he could have had them brought to her room and deposited in the wardrobe.

Fifteen minutes later she was dressed. Red satin flowed around her and she felt more elegant than she had ever felt before in her life. There had even been a selection of dainty slippers lining the bottom of the wardrobe. She put her hair back in a braid, fastening it in a loop on top of her head, wishing that her room had a shower or a bath. Her hair was stringy and greasy and in desperate need of a wash. It seemed like there was no indoor plumbing at all in this … wherever she was.  She had been using a chamber pot similar to the one at Gerwin and Elke's for the last few days.

Giselle marched in again, looked Christine over from head to toe, and nodded.

"That will do," she said, lips pursed in disapproval. "Follow me."

Christine followed Giselle obediently out of her room. They turned left and walked down a long hallway, dark except for some candles elaborately mounted on the wall in metal candelabras. Near the end of the hall, two staircases lined the walls, one ascending and one descending. They took the one on the left and it led down to a stylish entrance hall. Near the beginning of the hall was a door leading off to the right and there they entered the dining room.

Lord Radek sat at the head of the table and something about the scene seemed oddly familiar. He motioned for her to take a seat to his right. There were numerous chairs running down either side of the grand table. Christine walked with trepidation down to the seat Lord Radek had indicated and sat down.

"You look … lovely Christine," Lord Radek murmured seductively. "Normally I do not ask my … guests … to join me for dinner, but I could not resist the opportunity to spend some more time with you." He looked mockingly towards the door through which she had entered. "However, I do not think Giselle approves of my choice of dinner companion."

Christine glanced over and saw Giselle standing in the doorway. She had looked up just in time to see the stern look of disapproval on the woman's face swiftly change to abject horror as she scurried out. Apparently, Giselle was fearful of her employer.

"What exactly do you mean when you say that I'm your guest?" Christine asked, overcoming her own fear and daring to ask a direct question.

"Well, I am sure you have noticed some peculiarities about your current situation, hmmm?" Lord Radek's face seemed to hold a permanently mocking expression.

"Well, yes," Christine said. She paused and then decided that it was best to be direct. "I know that the fog had something to do with it. This isn't the same Thunder Bay that we left on Saturday." Christine mentally gasped as she realised that, by using the pronoun we, she had potentially given her sister away.

Lord Radek smiled as he correctly interpreted the flicker of horror that she had unsuccessfully tried to keep from her face. "Do not worry my dear. I know all about your sister. You will be happy to know that she is safe, for the moment. I am not completely certain for how long however, because she is keeping some questionable company."

"You've seen Sarah? Can I see her?" Christine was too shocked to hide her joy at finding out that her sister was okay.

"Well, as I said, I do not entirely approve of the company she is keeping. She was found by someone of whom I have been aware and watching for some time. He is a bit of a renegade in these parts and I actually should have taken care of him by now. I am really quite interested to see how the whole situation plays out, to tell you the truth."

"Who's she with? Is he dangerous? Do you think he'll hurt her?" Christine was frantic to obtain more information about her sister.

"I do not really know. That is the fascinating thing about Hillard. He seems to be fighting against his very nature. He does not seem to want to accept what he is."

"What do you *mean* by that? What is he?" Christine was confused.

Lord Radek sighed, lifted his glass, filled with a thick red liquid, and took a sip. "Well, my dear," he said, chuckling softly, "I am afraid that Hillard is a vampire." He looked up and his shining emerald eyes looked deeply into Christine's.

With those words, Christine realized why this room had seemed so familiar. She froze, her gaze locking with that of Lord Radek. The picture from the tapestry . . . The blood in the glasses . . . The man at the head of the table. It had been this room!

# Chapter 8

Sarah regained consciousness long before she opened her eyes. She remembered just enough from before she fainted to want to hang on to the comforting blanket of sleep that she was wrapped in. She knew that waking up would force her to remember, and she didn't want to face everything quite yet.

"Okay Sarah, I know you're awake. No use faking." Sarah recognised Hillard's voice and groaned.

"I don't want to wake up. I'm happier asleep." She didn't want to face all of the confusion she knew was waiting for her when she finally opened her eyes.

"And how are you supposed to help your sister if you're asleep? I thought you *wanted* to help her. You've been sleeping for two days." Hillard knew that the last bit would catch her attention.

Two days! Sarah's eyes flew open and she sat up quickly, and then just as abruptly lay back down. Her head was spinning.

"Okay, settle down," Hillard was still worried about her. He had considered giving her some of his blood, but waited to see if she would rally on her own. He had to admit though, he had been sorely tempted the night before. "I just wanted to get your attention. You've been pretty sick for the last few days. Last night I even wondered if you were going to make it until your fever broke."

Sarah had a vague memory of someone holding her hand, keeping her anchored to reality, as she drifted in and out of consciousness. She remembered dreams of being transported to another world, where Thunder Bay didn't exist and a castle stood at the top of Hillcrest Park. Was that a dream? She wasn't sure. That part was more vivid than the others. She remembered standing on the shore of Lake Superior, seeing the Sleeping Giant and turning back to see a castle. The castle where Christine was being held! It *hadn't* been a dream!

"Hillard? What's going on? How could any of this be possible?" she asked weakly, not really sure if she wanted to know the answer.

"I'm not really sure how to answer that right now. I mean, I know the answer, but I have to think about this for a bit. I can't have you fainting on me again. How about you let Adalaide give you some soup, and then you can show me that you're feeling better before we start throwing any more craziness at you. Okay?"

Sarah nodded. Part of her wanted to know the truth right now, but the other part of her just wanted to crawl back under the covers and pretend that she was at home safe and sound. Hillard looked at her intently for a moment, almost as if he wanted to come back and say something more, but instead he spun abruptly on his heel and left the room.

Sarah looked around the room. She was in a spacious, comfortable bed. The mattress was soft, if a bit lumpy, and there was a homemade quilt covering her. The other furniture in the room was also simple. There was a dresser, made of wood, and a small mirror that hung from the wall above it. A wooden brush and comb set rested on the dresser but nothing else cluttered its surface. There was a shelf on the wall opposite her bed, holding some knickknacks, mostly made of wood and carved to resemble animals. A wooden chair was positioned at the head of the bed, presumably so that Hillard and his friend could take care of her while she had been unconscious. There was also a single window and it had thick, heavy dark blue curtains which were now closed.

A tall redheaded woman entered the room at that moment and saw Sarah staring at the window. "I think you could use some light," she said, smiling. She laid the tray she had been carrying down on the dresser. Then she walked over to the window. She spread the curtains wide, allowing the bright sunshine outside to stream into the room, then turned and smiled at Sarah. "We were trying to keep things as dark and quiet for you as possible. You were very ill." The woman, who Sarah guessed was Adalaide, walked back to the dresser and brought the tray with the soup on it over to Sarah. Sarah tried to sit up again, but the dizziness was too intense, and she lay back down, sighing resignedly.

"No problem. I will feed you. You have not eaten anything for two days. I am not surprised if you feel a little dizzy. We shall get some food into you and then see how you are."

Sarah nodded gratefully. Her stomach was rumbling. Adalaide grabbed some extra pillows from the floor beside the dresser and helped to prop Sarah up into enough of a sitting position on the bed for her to eat. She stood back and looked Sarah, as if ascertaining whether her patient was really well enough to eat or was going to collapse into unconsciousness again. Finally she nodded to herself, apparently satisfied. She picked up the soup and sat down on the chair beside the bed.

She fed a few spoonfuls of soup to her patient. Sarah ate absently, still trying to understand what was going on. After a moment, Adalaide put the spoon back into the bowl. She looked at Sarah for a moment, seeing that she seemed to be lost in thought.

"Do you need some time by yourself?" she asked, as if she really understood the mess of chaotic thoughts that were whirling through Sarah's mind.

Sarah looked up at Adelaide gratefully. She really wasn't in the mood to be talking to anyone. What she really needed was some time alone to think. Adelaide tucked the bed covers around Sarah, making sure that she was safely sitting up in the bed, then handed the soup to her and left the room.

Sarah slowly sipped the delicious soup. It was a delightful vegetable mix - not hot enough to burn her mouth, but warm enough to sooth her still-irritated throat. It wasn't all that different from something she might have eaten back home when she was sick. Laying here, eating soup, she found it very hard to believe that there was anything out of the ordinary in her current situation.

Sarah finished her soup and lay back on the bed, pushing the extra pillows to the side. Her thoughts were tumultuous and wandering back and forth between worrying about her sister and trying to make sense of the differences between the surroundings in which she found herself and the Thunder Bay she knew. Her thoughts kept chasing themselves in circles and her tired brain eventually could not keep up anymore and she fell asleep.

When she awoke, she found Hillard once again sitting in the chair beside her bed. They just stared at each other intensely for several minutes before Hillard finally spoke.

"What do you know about vampires?"

Sarah was taken aback by the truly unexpected question. That was the last thing she had expected to hear when Hillard finally decided to explain to her what the hell was going on. There was a very long pause while Sarah contemplated how to answer before she finally spoke. Finally she took a deep breath and decided to just list what she knew, rather than try to figure out where Hillard was going with this bizarre line of questioning.

"Well, I know the stories started in Romania. And there was a book about Dracula, who was apparently the first of his kind."

Hillard smiled, seeming simultaneously relieved that she had recognized the word and amused at her use of the word story. "Well, I've never heard the story of Dracula. Are there any real vampires in your world?"

There it was – out in the open. This was *not* her world. Sarah focused on those last three words for a moment before actually processing the rest of the question.

"*Real* vampires? Well, I don't think so. Of course, there are always those people who read novels by people like Ann Rice because they find the idea of being outcast and undead very appealing. They seem to want to believe. But *real* vampires? No. I don't believe in them."

Hillard stared at her intently for a moment. "Well, that tells me something. What is the ruling structure like in your world?"

The phrase 'ruling structure' seemed like a strange way to describe politics. Sarah again had to think for a moment about how to answer before speaking.

"Well, I guess it depends on the country. Canada has a democratic system, as do a lot of countries in the world, to varying degrees. Some still have monarchies with kings and queens, and others have dictatorships with only one ruler. I think there are also a few ruled by various religious bodies."

"And are there many different countries?" Hillard asked.

"Of course," answered Sarah.

"And do you know of one called Deutschland?" Hillard spoke carefully.

Sarah paused for a moment. She didn't know any countries by that name, but it sounded vaguely familiar. It reminded her of her college years, when she was taking courses to be a medical secretary. But it clearly had nothing to do with medical terminology. The only other classes she had taken were her electives in Human Sexuality and her German course. German, of course! Deutschland was the word for Germany in the German language!

"Germany is what we call it in English, but yes, it's a country in Central Europe."

Now Sarah recognized the strange accent that pervaded Hillard's speech. German!

"Are you German?" asked Sarah.

Hillard smiled, "Almost everyone around here is." He stopped again for a moment, and then stood. "I must think about what you've told me before continuing," he said, "I'll return soon."

Sarah just stared after him as he walked out of the room. She felt more confused than ever now!

Christine just sat at the table and stared at Lord Radek. She didn't know how to react to his revelation that her sister was in the company of a supposed vampire. She was more shocked and horrified, however, to recognize the resemblance between the 'dinner' scene depicted on the tapestry in her room and the scene in which she now found herself. In fact, aside from the fact that the other guests were missing, she could almost imagine that she had stepped, in true Alice in Wonderland style, into the tapestry itself.

Lord Radek sipped the thick dark red substance from his glass and chuckled.

Christine didn't know how to respond to him at all. This situation was becoming more and more bizarre.

"A vampire? Are you kidding me?" she asked, unable to wrap her mind around the concept, or around what she saw even now right in front of her.

Lord Radek smiled. "Do you not believe in vampires, my dear?" he asked, his smile becoming a smirk. "Or is it that you have something against us as a species?"

Christine's eyes widened at his blatant assertion that he was also a vampire. She knew the myths of course, and the stories. She was even a bit of an Anne Rice fan, but to take it one step further and assert that the stories were true?! Part of her felt that, after the events of the past few days, it was entirely within this new realm of possibility she was trapped in. A much stronger part of her, however, insisted that she must deny what he was saying, and what she was thinking, in order to keep herself sane.

"At this point," she admitted, "I don't know what to believe. And, honestly, I thought I was invited down here for dinner. I don't want to talk about these things right now."

Lord Radek chuckled again. Christine felt like she was a never-ending source of amusement for him and she wanted nothing more than to leave and go back to her beautiful prison, even if it meant that she was alone again.

Various servants began bringing food into the room. Christine took a small portion of each dish; Lord Radek took none. Whenever he finished his glass of 'wine,' a servant brought him another.

Christine ate silently, barely tasting the food. She didn't want to think about Lord Radek's vampire comments, but found herself unable to think of anything else. Again, she considered the bizarre events of the past few days. Was the existence of vampires any more ridiculous than the existence of a fog that acted as some sort of gate between worlds? Finally, as she finished the food on her plate, Christine finally looked back over at Lord Radek only to find him studying her carefully – as he had presumably been doing the entire time she had been eating.

"Suppose I did believe in vampires?" She began cautiously. "Shouldn't I be horror-struck that my sister's with one? Or," she asserted, a reckless gleam in her eyes, "perhaps because I'm with one as well?" She waited to see Lord Radek's response, desperately hoping that she hadn't pushed him too far.

Lord Radek's green eyes, however, lit up with delight and he laughed quietly yet again.

"I knew you had intelligence, my Christine. I have felt how deeply your emotions run, but I fully admit that I have been more curious as to whether your brains match your beauty. Oh," he sighed, "you are so very tempting to me."

Christine didn't like the hungry gleam in his eyes. Even as a wave of indignation began to rise within her, she began to feel a sleepy sense of comfort blanket her. Before she was overwhelmed, however, she blurted out, "So, what, you're tempted to feed on me!? Is that right?"

Lord Radek stood up from his chair and went to stand behind Christine. She felt his hands on the back of her neck, then the brush of his fingertips as he brushed her curly blond hair aside to whisper in her ear. "Feed on you? That I have done many times, and you are sweet indeed. You tempt me to do so much more — things that are forbidden to me."

Christine wanted to move, to jump up from her chair and flee — flee this room, flee this castle, flee this world — but she was frozen. Part of her was screaming inside, but another part of her waited in eager anticipation for what would come next. It all felt familiar. Then she felt Lord Radek's sweet kiss on her neck and knew the truth. He *had* fed on her before; this was not the first time. And ... she liked it!

# Chapter 9

After Hillard had left the room, Sarah just stared at the door he had closed behind himself. He had provided her with very few answers – instead asking her more questions of his own. She mulled over those questions, trying to make some sort of sense out of what had just happened. Vampires? Germany? How were the two related? Germany was relatively close to Romania, but both were far, far away from Canada. Maybe she was not in some alternate universe. Maybe she was in some part of Germany. Maybe she had been kidnapped and taken half way across the world. To what end? Nothing made any sense.

Adalaide came back into the room, carrying another bowl of soup. "How is your stomach? Is it ready for a bit more nourishment? We need to try to get your strength up," she said brightly as she entered.

Sarah recognised that the soup she had eaten earlier was no longer making her stomach feel full. She could definitely eat again; her growling stomach was testament to that. She pushed herself into a more upright position, and was pleased to discover that the dizziness had abated.

Adalaide sat quietly beside Sarah as she ate. She looked as if she wanted to say something. After a few uncomfortable minutes of Sarah sipping on her soup and Adalaide simply sitting there staring at her, Sarah put down her spoon and looked directly at her hostess.

"What?" Sarah asked irritably. She knew that she should be nicer to Adelaide, who had helped to nurse her while she was sick, but she found herself annoyed by her just the same.

"I have never met a fog traveller before. What was it like? Did it hurt?"

Sarah just stared at Adalaide. "I have no idea. We were just driving. We drove through some fog. Sure, it was thicker than most fog, but it wasn't like we fell through some wormhole and ended up in outer space. The only difference I noticed was that the road wasn't paved anymore."

Adalaide nodded, but from her confused expression, Sarah got the idea that Adalaide hadn't understood everything that she had said. Adalaide had a thicker German accent than Hillard did and Sarah had the idea that she didn't speak a lot of English. She made a mental note to speak in more simple terms with her and to be careful to speak a bit more slowly.

"Is this your house?" Sarah asked. She figured that it was, but it seemed polite to make conversation with someone who was feeding her and who had been apparently taking care of her for three days.

"Yes. I was born here. I have lived here all my life."

There was a knock at the door and Adelaide looked up, with what looked like an expression of regret on her face at being interrupted while getting to know her guest. Hillard peeked in.

"Can I come in?" He sounded almost like a little kid, asking permission to come sit with the adults.

"Of course," said Sarah. "I want to finish our conversation as soon as possible. I have to admit that I'm more confused now than ever."

Hillard chuckled a little. "I'm not surprised. You're the first person I've had this discussion with. I've seen other fog travellers, of course, and spoken to a few, but this is the first time I've tried to explain all of this to anyone. I don't want to make things any more confusing for you than they already are."

This surprised Sarah a bit. She wondered where he had learned to speak English. She had assumed that he had learned by speaking with other people like herself. She asked, timidly, "If you and everyone else around here is German, why do you all speak English?"

"Well," he answered, seeming relieved to be asked a slightly less complicated question, "when the fog travellers come through, they don't all speak German, of course. As children, we're taught several of the main languages in school so that we can communicate. I'm pretty fluent in English and French, as well as my native German."

Sarah was amazed that he knew so many languages. She had been forced to learn a bit of French in school as a child, but would never consider herself to be fluent in anything except English. Although she was curious about the type of schooling the children here received, she decided to turn the conversation back to what was really on her mind.

"So, have you come back with more questions for me," she asked, unable to keep the note of sarcasm out of her voice, "or are you finally going to start answering some of mine?"

He nodded. "I know it hasn't been fair to you. It's just difficult to explain if I don't understand the differences between our two worlds. I want to give you an explanation that makes sense to you."

"Well, you haven't done a very good job of it so far," she exclaimed in frustration.

"Okay, let me just clarify a few more things. I promise not to walk away again without explaining everything, okay?" Hillard's bright green eyes looked pleadingly into her own. She found it hard to resist his earnest expression.

"Okay. Fine. Does that mean you have *more* questions for me?" Sarah tried to remain patient with Hillard, but it was difficult facing the prospect of answering more of *his* questions when she had so many of her own burning within her brain.

"Yes. First, what do you know of the history of the country you call Germany?"

"Well, I know that they have been in a lot of wars over the years. In fact, they tried to take over other countries several times in the past. I know that they were the main cause of World War II and a leading player in World War I. I don't know a lot about what happened before then, though." Sarah wondered where this was all going to lead.

"Well, that's a start. Our … Germany … here has had a long history of war with other … countries. About five hundred years ago, there were many small wars between different groups in that country. One leader came to the forefront, his name was Charles the fifth. Do you know that name?" Hillard looked searchingly at Sarah.

"I've heard of leaders named Charles in the past, but I have to say that I don't have a lot of knowledge of history," Sarah admitted.

"Well, our Charles the fifth stood out in many ways. He fought many battles, always coming out victorious. What really made him famous, however, was the fact that he received many supposedly mortal wounds, yet always managed to survive. In fact, he quickly gained a reputation of being almost immortal."

"The how of the matter is unknown now, at least it is to me. But Charles somehow became infected with vampirism. He essentially *was* immortal. No one was his match on the battle field. And it soon became obvious that many of his soldiers were obtaining his same abilities."

Hillard paused for a moment and Sarah let her mind run back over what he had been saying. She found it interesting the way Hillard had said that Charles became *infected* with vampirism, almost as if it were a disease.

He began again. "Sarah, what do you know about vampires?" He looked almost afraid to hear her answer.

She waited a moment before answering, then began to list the traits that were commonly discussed when the topic of vampires was brought up. She felt kind of ridiculous, listing off a bunch of what she had always thought was superstitious nonsense.

"Hmmm. They don't like garlic. Holy water burns them. The sign of the cross scares them away. Their reflection can't be seen in mirrors. And they can be killed by shoving a wooden stake through their heart, or by lighting them on fire. Sunlight will kill them as fast as fire. And, of course, they drink human blood."

Hillard looked amused through the recitation of most of her list, but the last item caused a pensive look to pass over his face. He paused a moment, thinking before he spoke again.

"Well, most of that isn't true. They have a history of war with the church, but holy water and crosses have no effect on them. They also have no problems with garlic. A wooden stake doesn't kill them, but can paralyze them if placed properly, and if they catch on fire they will burn until nothing is left. Finally, while they can't stay in the sun for long periods without becoming very weak, sunlight doesn't kill them."

Sarah stared at him blankly. "So what you're trying to tell me is that vampires are real?"

He took a deep breath. "Yes, Sarah. And your sister is being held by one."

She shook her head. She felt like her heart was beating too fast.. She was also having trouble breathing and it had nothing to do with her cold. "I don't want to hear any more of this. I think I need to rest. I just need to sleep for a bit." She pulled the covers up to her chin and rolled over, her back towards Hillard. She heard him sigh.

"Okay, Sarah. I understand. I'll be in the other room if you want to talk some more. I want to answer all of your questions, but I understand that you need some time to process all of this." She heard the door shut quietly behind him as he left the room.

Sarah tried to block her conversation with Hillard out of her mind. This was all just too much to deal with. How much craziness was one person supposed to be able to handle? How was she supposed to just accept everything at face value when it all went against everything she knew logically?

She lay in the bed for over an hour, trying to both block everything out and find the escape of sleep, but was successful with neither. Even though most of her mind resisted any idea of this being real at all, a tiny voice inside her head told her that she *had* to accept this, that it *was* real, and that her sister was depending on her.

Sarah thought about her sister then. If all of this were true, then Christine was in grave danger, if she was even still alive. Sarah knew that she had to get out of bed, pull herself together, and do something to help Christine – but to do that she would have to take a leap of faith, perhaps a leap into madness. She felt so weak and tired – both mentally and physically. If she weren't still so ill, maybe she could think more clearly. It seemed like everything just fell apart all at once – the destruction of her marriage, her illness, the fog, the craziness.

Suddenly, without any conscious effort on Sarah's part, her mind found a way to accept the unacceptable. Perhaps none of this was real after all. Maybe she was laying in a bed somewhere, delirious from a fever. In which case, it didn't matter if it were real or not, she could get out of bed and play along. Part of her felt like, no matter if this were real or not, she *had* to help her sister. She and Christine had been through too much together – their father's alcoholism, their mother's slow death from cancer – for her to leave Christine alone, even if this *was* just delirium.

Sarah made a conscious decision to play along with Hillard, no matter how unbelievable this all was and she finally sat up in bed and swung her legs over the side. So, vampires were real, were they? Well, she would be going in opposition to one to save her sister. She needed all of the information she could get to prepare herself. It was time to find her key source of information – Hillard.

---

Christine awoke the next morning back in the beautiful prison that was her room. She had a hard time remembering anything at all at first, but then the images of Lord Radek kissing [biting!] her neck came back to her all too clearly. He had drunk her blood! He'd been drinking her blood for days! That would explain her lethargy, her inexplicable weakness. She thought carefully over the events of the past few days. Last night had been the third time she remembered that [exquisite] kiss on her neck. A vampire! As if finding herself in another world were not enough! She had to find a way to escape from here. Gervis had seemed so eager to help her, but Christine hadn't seen him since Lord Radek's return to the Castle days ago. She hoped that he was okay, that Lord Radek hadn't punished him too harshly. She decided to ask Giselle about him the next time she saw her.

Christine got up out of the bed and realized that she was no longer in her beautiful scarlet gown, but was now dressed back in the cotton nightgown she had been wearing since she arrived. She was happy to see that at least it was now clean and no longer smelled of old sweat. One thought struck her though – who had changed her clothing last night? Christine hoped it had been Giselle and not Lord Radek. The thought of him caressing her unconscious naked body nauseated her.

There was a brief knock on the door and then Giselle entered the room. This was the first time she had ever knocked before coming in and she seemed more subdued than her normally haughty self. Christine remembered the look of fear on Giselle's face when Lord Radek had chastised her the night before. Perhaps Christine's situation in the castle was improving. If Lord Radek was treating her differently than the other visitors he'd had before, it was possible that it could provide her with an opportunity. Perhaps, if she played her cards right, she could find a way to escape.

She looked thoughtfully at Giselle as she placed the breakfast tray on the dressing table and began busily making Christine's bed.

"Giselle, I know you don't like me, but I want to ask you a question."

Giselle turned to her, a look of surprise on her face at having been spoken to. Just as quickly, the look turned to suspicion. "I won't be helping you to leave this place," she snapped at Christine.

Christine thought carefully before she spoke. "I don't want to leave. I feel safe here. Lord Radek has explained that he just wants to take care of me. And I have everything I could ever want or need."

"Then what's the question you want me to be answering?" The suspicious look on Giselle's face only increased.

"Well, I haven't seen Gervis since my first night here. I know I mustn't see or speak to him, but I want to make sure he's okay. I don't want to cause him any more trouble by asking Lord Radek."

The suspicious look on Giselle's face softened for a moment and then hardened again before she answered. "He's getting better now. Lord Radek drained him near to death out of anger at his treachery. If it weren't for the pact he has with Gervis' parents, that fine young man would be dead right now, thanks to you!"

Giselle straightened the covers on Christine's bed with a final, abrupt tug and then she stormed out of the room, first slamming, and then locking the door behind her.

Christine pondered this new bit of information. At least Gervis was still alive. But this meant she could not depend on him for rescue. In fact, she decided firmly, she would follow Giselle's initial advice and avoid any contact with him at all. She really liked him and would deeply regret it if any lasting harm came to him because of her. It appeared that she was on her own.

Sarah opened the door to her room and peeked out into the rest of the cottage. Having been unconscious when she arrived, she was curious as to the appearance of the rest of the dwelling.

There appeared to be only one other room. It was bigger than her bedroom, with a makeshift wooden divider blocking a small part of the room off and the rest open. There was a wood-burning stove to her left, with a wooden shelf providing counter space beside it. There was a comfortable-looking couch on the other side of the stove, made of wood and covered with pillows, and a wooden table, surrounded by four chairs, right beside a thick wooden door that appeared to lead outside. Sarah saw Adalaide and Hillard sitting at the table, deep in discussion. From what she could hear, they were speaking in German. The conversation broke off as Hillard noticed Sarah peeking at them.

"You okay?" he asked, concern on his face.

"Yeah. I have more questions," she said, realizing that she had so many questions at the moment that she didn't even know where to start.

"Want some more soup?" Adalaide offered.

Sarah nodded absently as she sat down at the table, still trying to wade through the myriad of questions swirling around in her brain. Adalaide walked over to the old-fashioned woodstove and spooned some soup out of a pot resting on top.

"Are you feeling any better?" Hillard asked, obviously aware that Sarah was not yet ready to begin with her questions.

"I feel tired and a bit weak, but better," she admitted, trying still to maintain some of the illusion in her own mind that this was all some kind of fever delusion. She slowly sipped the soup that Adalaide had placed before her on the table.

Hillard spoke after a few moments. "Adalaide is going to go to the castle in a little while to ask around about your sister."

Sarah looked gratefully at Adelaide. "Can I come?" she asked eagerly.

Hillard shook his head. "Not a good idea Sarah. We don't know how much Lord Radek knows about you. We wouldn't want to have you trapped in there with your sister. Plus, in your weakened state, you're in no shape for the walk there. Give it least a few more hours before you decide to run out to rescue your sister." He smiled at her, reassuringly. "Don't worry. I don't think she's in any danger at the moment. We'll get to her before anything bad happens."

Sarah felt some relief at his words and had to admit that he was right about her health, but her instinct was to jump up,  march over to the castle and demand that this Lord Radek release her sister immediately. She had to agree with Hillard, however, she'd probably pass out in the woods before she even got within sight of the castle.

"Who *is* this Lord Radek?" she asked.

"He is the self-proclaimed Lord of these parts," Hillard explained. "He is the Vampire Lord. All of our cities and towns are ruled by vampires, but most are not as cruel, nor as crazy, as Lord Radek has proved himself to be over the years."

"Your people are ruled by vampires?" Sarah was confused. This didn't sound much like the stories she had heard about vampires in her world. Those vampires lived in castles, sure, but they avoided people for the most part.

"I explained earlier that Charles the Fifth was the first vampire and that he created a vampire army for himself, remember?"

"Yes."

Hillard paused, and Sarah stood up as Adelaide appeared, ready to leave. Adelaide hugged her, slung a knapsack over one shoulder, and left the cottage. Sarah mentally wished her good luck as she watched Adelaide march into the forest through the window. She hoped that Adelaide would return with some good news about her sister. Then, finally tearing her eyes away from the window, she turned back to Hillard with a look of expectation in her eyes. After a moment, he continued.

"Well, over the next fifty years, Charles the Fifth managed to unite all of the German leaders under his rule. At the same time, other world leaders had become infected by vampirism. The King of France, Francis the First, and the King of England, Henry the Eighth, were the most notable. Those two had begun a war during the 1530's that was beginning to rage throughout Europe, involving huge vampire armies."

Sarah just sat quietly, listening to Hillard, enthralled by this alternate history.

"At that time, the numbers of vampires had swelled to enormous, nearly unsustainable proportions. One side, lead by Francis the first, felt that it was their right, ordained by God, to rule the Earth. They were starting to believe that they were gods themselves and that the humans were merely cattle for them to consume at will. The other side was lead by the more pragmatic

Henry the Eighth, who felt that religion held no part of the vampire existence, but felt that the Earth should fall under his leadership alone."

"It was at this time that one of Francis the First's high councillors, called DaVinci, decided that it was time to take matters into his own hands. He could see the devastation that was occurring as well as the inevitable outcome – the extinction of the human race."

Sarah gasped in recognition. "Leonardo DaVinci?"

"Yes, you know of him?"

"Yeah, he was a wonderful artist and inventor in my world. He was a vampire?" Christine was stunned, but in a way she wasn't that surprised. DaVinci was a very colourful historic figure, and he was known to be a dominant figure in many historical conspiracy theories. Being a vampire as well was not really that huge a leap.

"In this world DaVinci was converted to vampirism by Francis the First himself. Francis was intrigued by DaVinci's ideas and inventiveness. But, somewhere along the way, that freedom of thought led DaVinci's beliefs down a road that was different from that of Francis. DaVinci recognized that the vampires needed to develop a more symbiotic relationship with the humans, rather than one of pure dominance. He saw the only survival of the vampire race as coming from a culling of their numbers. He had a large number of followers himself, and joining forces with the army of Charles the Fifth, they determined to somehow cull the numbers and bring some sort of peace to the vampire race. The battle between the Symbiots and the Dictators lasted for nearly a century. DaVinci's vision of culling the numbers of the vampire race was satisfied during the war, but at the expense of nearly all of his followers. Near the end, it is said that DaVinci fled into the mountains in the Far East."

Sarah was so enthralled by the story that she hadn't even realized that Hillard had stopped for a moment and was watching her face with a speculative look. She wondered how it must seem to him, telling this story to someone who had never heard it before. She wondered how he felt about her intense interest.

Hillard took a deep breath and continued. "You should know that the vampire race was not the only casualty of the Great Vampire War. The human race was also decimated in the process. Vampiric healing takes a great deal of energy, and humans were used as the main power source to continue the war. The rumour is that DaVinci, while against the mentality of both Francis and Henry, saw the beauty of the vampire and did not want the race to be completely destroyed. On the other hand, he also knew the beauty of humankind as well. He feared that the human race would be extinguished and tried to find some way to increase their numbers. It was while DaVinci was in the eastern mountains that the fogs began. Humans came through the fog – not every time, but often enough to begin to replenish the numbers for a time – *if* the vampiric numbers remained low. These fogs occurred in places scattered all over the world, and on a fairly regular schedule. To this day, no one knows exactly what causes them – at least no one I've ever spoken to. All that is known is that the people who come through the fog are from worlds similar to our own, but they don't always come from the same world. That's how you came to be here."

Sarah just stared at Hillard for a moment. There had been a few disappearances on the road from Thunder Bay to the United States over the years. Of course, it was also a common route for drug runners, so not all of the disappearances would necessarily have been reported.

A thought struck her then. Had she and Christine been brought here as food?

"We're supposed to be food?" she asked, unbelievingly.

Hillard smiled wistfully at her. "Not necessarily. You were brought here to replenish and strengthen the human numbers on this world. Some vampires see that as simply food replacement, but others see it as an opportunity to learn about other worlds and technologies."

"How did DaVinci create the fog?" Sarah asked. She had never heard of any technology like that. She *was* a bit of a science fiction buff, so she guessed that the parallel worlds were something like those suggested in the old television series Quantum Leap – where infinite worlds existed in parallel to our own, the only difference being that at some point in time a different choice had been made. For example, in another world, she and Christine might have decided to drive to Winnipeg instead of to the spa in the United States. They would still be in that world, because they never would have encountered the fog. Or someone else might have come through the fog. If so, where were those other people? The infinite possibilities were giving her a headache.

"No one knows how he did it – or even *if* it was really him. He was just thought of as the most likely suspect because of his intense studies in science, magic, and technology, and his interest in replenishing the human race."

Sarah stared into space for a few moments, trying to take it all in. Here was a world history very different from her own.

"And is DaVinci still alive?" she asked.

"No one knows that, either. The histories say that he never came down from the mountains. Charles the Fifth declared him dead after a year or two and declared himself to be the victor in the war. A few good things resulted from the Great Vampire War, despite the great destruction involved. First, the numbers of vampires were greatly depleted, leaving just over a thousand still in existence. Also, the human race was able to begin to grow again. Finally, both Francis and Henry came to realize that a more manageable power structure was required, because immediately after the Great Vampire War they began to explore the world. Other continents were discovered, with more humans to feed on. Charles the Fifth decided to form the Vampire Council – with him at the head – which would act as world rulers. Most vampires still saw themselves as gods, you see, and felt that it was their *right* to rule the world. The members of the Vampire Council are like the ultimate gods, to whom every other vampire must answer. The Council quickly decreed that the making of new vampires was forbidden without their permission. Any new vampires created without this permission would be immediately destroyed, along with their creators. In that way, Charles ended up fulfilling DaVinci's vision."

"So is there still a Council?" asked Sarah.

"Yes, and Charles the Fifth is still at its head. Other vampires have tried to challenge him over the years, but have failed, unable to match the power of the oldest known vampire."

"Does that mean that they get stronger with age?"

"Apparently so. Although some also think that it's related to the amount of blood consumed. For that reason, whenever someone challenges Charles, there is usually a human massacre somewhere in the world first. The Council watches for just such occurrences."

"So human beings are just cattle for these monsters!?" The story was starting to lose its appeal as Sarah started to focus again on the human role in this world.

"Not so. Over time, the Council developed methods to create blood sustainability. Blood is our main form of currency, measured in Geschenk – which originally meant 'gift' in German. Each vampire rules their own area – often a few towns or a city – and they collect yearly taxes from all of their citizens who have reached adulthood. Several people travel to a Blood Bank every day and provide blood there. The blood is then stored chilled in glass tubes, with a few herbs added to decrease the clotting effect, and the Lord consumes them within a day or so. Each citizen who owns land is required to make this sort of contribution once a year. They also have the ability to go to the Blood Bank to provide Geschenk up to three more times a year, which can then be used as currency to buy food, supplies, or whatever is available. Each Geschenk can be divided into one hundred Stück. Citizens use Stück to pay for food and clothing and other necessities. It's the Vampire Lord's job to keep his or her citizens happy and healthy so that the population is sufficient to provide for his or her needs."

Sarah was amazed that an entire monetary system had been developed based on the vampiric need for blood. It didn't sound nearly as evil as the vampire novels of her own world made it sound. In fact, it actually sounded as if there were no reason in this world for anyone to be homeless or to go hungry.

"It doesn't sound as bad as I thought it would," she admitted.

"It isn't, if the Vampire Lord runs his land the way he's supposed to, as set out in the Vampire Code. In fact, it can provide a comfortable existence for many. The problem here in Donner is that Lord Radek is *not* following the Code. He keeps a number of humans in his castle as a constant food supply. Instead of receiving his Geschenk as deposited in the Blood Bank, freely given, he often takes the blood forcibly from his victims."

Sarah realized suddenly what Hillard was telling her. "So Christine is being held in the castle as his food?"

Hillard nodded grimly. "Yes, and we need to rescue her soon. Lord Radek's victims rarely last more than a few weeks before they are too weak from blood loss to survive."

Sarah abruptly got up from the table, walked over to the door, and stared outside for awhile, almost willing Adalaide to appear with news about her sister. She knew, however, that it would be hours before Adalaide returned.

"So," she asked finally, sitting back down across from Hillard, "how do we rescue my sister from this monster?"

"I'll think of something," he said reassuringly. "Adalaide and I have many friends inside the castle."

"Do you think Christine is being treated all right?" Sarah shook her head at the ridiculous question and then restated, "Well, aside from the fact that he's drinking her blood?"

"I don't know. I've never seen any of Lord Radek's victims after they've been taken to the castle, and I've never asked anyone who works there. Sometimes it's just easier not to know."

Sarah looked over at Hillard in surprise. "Why are you helping me then? If you've never helped anyone before, why do it now?"

Hillard's intense green eyes stared into her own for a moment and then he looked away quickly before saying quietly, "I like you Sarah." He looked at her again and smiled. "I think it was the angry look on your face when you were beating on that car horn. You looked so determined and angry. I liked that fire you showed."

Sarah blushed and looked down at the table. She *was* known for being as stubborn as a mule sometimes. She looked back up at Hillard and smiled back at him. "I like you too. I don't know what I would've done without you."

Hillard felt very drawn to Sarah. In some ways, she seemed very fragile, and in others she was as stubborn as an old horse. He did like her very much, especially when she smiled at him like she was doing right now. He just had to remember to keep his distance. Above all else, he needed to keep her safe, and part of that meant not letting her get too close.

Trying to change the subject, Sarah asked, "Why does the Vampire Council let Lord Radek to get away with breaking the rules?"

"Well," replied Hillard, "the lands of different Vampire Lords are far apart from each other. Communication between different lands is rare.  There is some trade, carried out by independent merchant groups."

"I guess that explains why my cell phone didn't work," Sarah smiled ruefully.

"Yes. I've seen other fog travellers carrying that kind of technology, but we have nothing close to it here. We can send letters and messages with the travelling merchants, but Lord Radek has an agreement with them. They are paid well to ensure that no negative messages about Lord Radek get through."

Something struck Sarah strange at that point. "If the vampires live so far away from each other, how can the Vampire Council meet and tell the rest of the vampires their decisions, especially those across the ocean?"

"That is some kind of vampire secret, but I think it must be some type of mental communication. They have many mysterious powers." Hillard didn't like keeping things from Sarah, but he didn't want to appear too knowledgeable about the vampires, in case that aroused her suspicions.

The mention of mysterious powers caught Sarah's interest.  It would be important to learn as much as she could about the strengths of Lord Radek before she went after him.  "What other powers do they have?" she asked eagerly.

"The most important, and the most dangerous," said Hillard, "is their ability to affect human emotion. They can't control your thoughts, but they *can* implant false feelings of security in their victims – or increase their terror a hundred times."

Sarah thought about that for a moment. No wonder the vampires were able to maintain control. Any time a human came near, meaning them harm, the threatened vampire could theoretically transform any feelings of hostility into safety. "Can they do it to more than one person at a time?" she asked curiously.

"Yes, normally. As long as the vampire is not in a weakened state, they can control anyone within their range of sight. If they are weakened, however, by a need to heal or a prolonged exposure to sunlight, they could have difficulty controlling even a single person."

"So that's a weakness we could exploit," Sarah suggested eagerly.

"Yes. That's what I've been thinking. And we have a secret weapon, as well. For some reason, there are a few individuals who are immune to the emotional influence of the Vampire Lords. I happen to be one of them." Hillard felt uncomfortable telling Sarah this lie, even though it was just a lie of omission. Again he told himself that was safer if she didn't know. He didn't know how she would react if she found out he was one of those 'monsters' they had been discussing.

Sarah's eyes lit up. "Seriously? So we actually have a chance of rescuing Christine! This could actually work!"

Hillard tried to temper Sarah's enthusiasm. "Just remember, Lord Radek is a very old, very powerful vampire. He has been ruling this Land for more than two hundred years and drinks much more blood than the average vampire."

Sarah's eyes widened. "Does he drink more than just the Geschenk and the fog travellers?"

"Yes," Hillard replied grimly. "He drains any criminal. No matter what the crime – stealing a piece of bread or killing another man – the punishment is always the same."

Sarah was shocked. "He would kill someone even for stealing food for their family?"

"Oh, yes. He sees it as one more excuse to increase his blood consumption."

"He really *is* a monster! He needs to be stopped!"

"Yes, but that's not an easy thing to do. It's been tried many times and no one has ever succeeded. For now, let's just focus on rescuing your sister."

"I know. But what happens after we rescue her? Can we go back and wait for the fog to come again so we can go home?"

Hillard shook his head ruefully. "It doesn't work that way Sarah," he said, his voice thick with regret. "You never know which world you would be going to.  The only constant is that the fog always comes here.  If you tried to go back through it, you would most likely only end up trapped in another world that isn't your own."

Sarah thought about that for a moment. "But we could escape Lord Radek that way."

Hillard considered that. "True. In fact, that would probably be the safest option for you two after we rescue Christine. The only problem would be keeping you safe until the next fog."

"How often do they come?"

"Once a month, with the full moon. So, we would have to hide you for about three weeks. I have some friends who could give us food, but we'll have to hide in the woods."

Sarah could see their plan slowly developing. Now they just needed Adalaide to return with some information about Christine.

# Chapter 10

Christine spent most of the next day sleeping. She hoped that she could regain her strength enough to try to escape in a few days. She ate and drank everything that Giselle brought her, smiling brightly at the woman every time she arrived, hoping that her friendly overtures would soften Giselle's harsh demeanour towards her.

During the times when she was awake, Christine examined her room more thoroughly. She looked through the clothing in the closet for something more appropriate for an escape attempt than a ball gown or night gown. Surprisingly, at the back corner of the wardrobe, folded neatly, she found her own clothing. Instead of putting them on, however, she left them where they were, deciding that it was more important for her to continue her subterfuge of being overwhelmed and swayed by the opulence of the castle.

The dressing table held no further information for her, and Christine shuddered every time she happened to glance over at the macabre tapestry on the wall.

Looking out the window, however, did provide a bit more insight into the area. The castle was located at the top of a high hill, with smaller cottages scattered below, between the hill and the great body of water that she recognised as Lake Superior. She could see people walking between the buildings and she longed to be out there with them. She hoped that once she escaped she would be able to find someone who knew the whereabouts of her sister.

Thinking about her own experiences with Lord Radek, she hoped that Sarah was okay. While she was happy to hear that Sarah wasn't alone, she was worried that if Lord Radek had been telling her the truth about this Hillard character, then Sarah could be in just as much trouble as she was.

Christine examined the door to her prison carefully. She saw no way for her to pick the lock (she had only ever seen such things on television) and the hinges were on the other side. She went back over to the wall containing the secret door and inspected it carefully. She could see where the door was, now that she knew it was there, but could find no hidden switch or lever to open it. Finally, in frustration, she slammed her fists against the wall letting out a cry of aggravation, no longer caring if Lord Radek could hear her. If she couldn't get out of the room, there would be no escape.

"Christine? Are you okay?" a voice whispered through the door to her room. She recognised the voice as Gervis' and, while elated that the one person sympathetic to her cause was so near, she was afraid of causing him any more trouble. She rushed over to the door and pressed her ear against the hard, impenetrable wood.

"Gervis? You shouldn't be here," she whispered.

"I only have a moment, but I have to tell you that Lord Radek will be leaving the castle tonight to search for your sister. I will come to you then and help you to escape."

"But Gervis, you'll get in trouble. Lord Radek might kill you this time."

She heard Gervis' heavy sigh through the door. "I'm coming with you Christine. I can't do this any more. Lord Radek is keeping me here as a form of control over my parents. We can go and get them and all escape to somewhere else."

"But my sis..." Christine broke off as she heard footsteps approaching. She heard Gervis scramble quickly away from the door. It sounded like another man had approached from downstairs. Christine was relieved that it wasn't Giselle, not wanting to feel the brunt of the woman's wrath again. Pleasantries were exchanged and the other man didn't sound suspicious at all. After a moment, Christine was relieved to hear two sets of footsteps retreating down the hall.

Christine was relieved that she would finally have a way to escape her room. But how could she possibly leave the castle now? Lord Radek was going after her sister! The last thing she wanted was to be free outside the castle and have her sister trapped in here.

Sarah and Hillard spent the rest of the day talking. She learned about the many differences between this blood-based society and her own.

She quickly reasoned out why the level of technology in this world was so far beneath her own. It seemed that the Geschenk kept the people fairly weak and that the average life span was still only fifty years. It was difficult for people to be creative and innovative when daily life was a struggle. In addition, the Vampire Lords discouraged innovation, feeling threatened and worried that the humans might find a way to overcome their rule. The lack of communication prevented the exchange of ideas that was so important to technological advancement. Technology in this world had barely advanced from the level that had existed during the fifteenth century. It made Sarah see so clearly how much her own world depended on technology – the telephone, computers, even plumbing and running water – and how much she had always taken it for granted.

However, while the Vampire Lords stifled innovation, they obviously realized the value of at least a basic education. Children went to school from the age of six to sixteen, learning reading, writing and basic mathematics, as well as several languages. In addition, they also learned about the ruling system, called "Blood Governance" and basic information about the key trades that could be learned in the area.

Once a child turned sixteen, parents could pay for their child to serve as an apprentice and learn a trade, or teach them a trade themselves if they were so skilled. The other option, if a family couldn't afford the apprenticeship fees, was for the child to join their Vampire Lord's household as a guard or house servant. By joining the Lord's household, they wouldn't have to pay their one Geschenk a year, which they could do only after turning eighteen anyway, because they didn't own any land. They would also be fully provided with food and clothing. In this way, someone who wanted to buy land and build a house on it, could do so after saving for a year or two. Another option was to learn a trade in an apprenticeship and then serve in the Vampire Lord's castle for a year or two to save enough Geschenk to build their own shop or farm.

Geschenk could be earned by going to the bank and giving a Geschenk of blood up to four times a year – including any yearly Geschenk fee. A full Geschenk could not be given more than once every three months, or the person giving would be weakened to a point where they could be vulnerable to illness. In that way, everyone between the ages of eighteen and fifty were guaranteed a yearly income of four Geschenk, or four hundred Stück. One person could theoretically live on such an amount, but Stück, being traded for goods as well, could also be earned through one's trade. A trade, or some other way to earn extra income, was necessary if you wanted a family, however, since children couldn't earn Geschenk themselves.

It was all very interesting to Sarah, but she was hoping that they would not be staying in this world, with its dependence on blood, for very long.

"Hillard," she suggested, shyly. "Why don't you come with us? You said yourself that you're a wanderer. Come wander with us for awhile."

The truth was, she didn't want to say goodbye to Hillard. She liked being around him. Besides being handsome — she was especially fond of his emerald eyes — he was smart and had a sweet sense of humour. She knew he probably wasn't interested in her romantically, but she wanted his friendship, if nothing else. She wasn't really interested in a relationship with *anyone* right now. It hadn't even been a week since she'd caught her bastard of a husband cheating on her with their neighbour, and she wasn't about to make the same mistake again. For some reason, she just wasn't good enough for any man. Even before her jackass husband, her prior boyfriends had all had a habit of cheating on her. She'd thought things with Paul had been different, because he'd married her, but they obviously hadn't been. Whether it was her flabby thighs, big behind, or something else, she obviously wasn't good enough for a real relationship with anyone.

Sarah realized then that her mind had wandered off and Hillard hadn't answered her question. He was just staring at her, with a wistful look on his face. He met her eyes and shook his head slowly.

"I can't Sarah. I would love to — I really would — but I have other commitments here."

Sarah's mind automatically went to Adalaide and she felt a blush crawling up her face. Of course he wouldn't come with them! He had Adalaide, with her long legs, firm stomach, and stunningly long red hair. There was no way that Sarah could ever compete with that. She should have guessed, but her hopeful mind had been working overtime again, seeing meaningful glances and gentle touches between herself and Hillard as something other than concerned friendship.

Hillard saw Sarah's face turn red and knew that she had come to some faulty assumption. He wanted to correct her, to tell her that he would love to go with her, to spend more time with her, but he had important things he had to finish here first. Plus, he could never risk introducing vampirism into another world, no matter how dedicated he was to never siring another of his kind himself.

Adalaide came rushing in at that moment, breaking up the tension. "Lord Radek is coming out to look for you tomorrow," she gasped, breathing heavily. It was obvious that she'd been running. "We have to get you out of here! He knows you are with Hillard and he also knows that Hillard and I are friends, so he is sure to come here to look for you!"

Sarah looked over at Hillard, forgetting about the tense moment earlier, and saw from his expression that he was thinking the same thing that she was.

"If he's out here looking for you," Hillard said, a mischievous glint in his green eyes, "then we should go into his castle to find your sister."

The three of them began discussing potential plans. Adalaide insisted that they get Sarah out of the cottage immediately, because Lord Radek wasn't known for his patience or for giving accurate accounts of his plans to his house servants. Adalaide had also heard about the problems that had occurred with Gervis because of his involvement with Christine, but didn't mention them as she didn't want to provide Sarah with any more reasons to worry about her sister.

They quickly packed up some food and left the cottage, heading north-west. The castle was to the south-west of Adelaide's cottage, but Adalaide said that she had a place where they could hide overnight and resupply.

Hillard just nodded when Adalaide mentioned the hideout, and Sarah realized that he already knew about it. She felt a flash of jealousy at their obviously close relationship but suppressed it, reminding herself that she was just friends with Hillard, after all.

It took them almost three hours of hiking through the bush to reach the hiding place. Sarah was exhausted when they finally reached it, but Hillard and Adalaide had done all of the carrying and had kept to a very slow pace, keeping in mind that Sarah had been very ill for the last few days and had not had much time to recover.

Sarah almost had to stop a few times, but the thought of the monstrous Lord Radek catching her before she could rescue her sister kept her going. When they finally stopped walking, Sarah was confused for a moment. She didn't see anything that looked even remotely habitable, not even a rabbit hole.

Adalaide walked to a small space between a cluster of trees and reached down into some brush. Sarah was amazed when a door, big enough for a person to pass through, opened into the ground. Stairs led down into darkness, and Adalaide lit a candle before venturing down the stairway, motioning for Hillard and Sarah to follow. Sarah was glad for the dim candle light when Hillard pulled the door closed behind them.

The stairs descended for a short distance and then opened up into a rather large dug-out room.  There was a bed against one wall, a shelf containing various foodstuffs and, Sarah was astonished to see, an entire wall covered with a vast assortment of swords, axes and other weapons.

"You seem prepared to go to war," Sarah said, trepidation in her voice. She didn't know what, exactly, she had expected Adalaide's hideaway to look like, but she hadn't expected this!

Adalaide just smiled grimly over at Sarah. "Lord Radek and I are not the best of friends. I expected that I would need a place to hide from him at some point or another."

When it appeared that Adalaide wasn't going to expand on that revelation, Sarah decided to just help a bit with the unpacking. She sat down on the bed and helped to go through Hillard's pack, taking out his tin dishes and blankets. Hillard spread his thick canvas ground cover on the floor of the room and began making a bed for himself. Adalaide pulled a chest out from under the bed, removed some thick woollen blankets, and began making a sleeping place for herself beside him.

"I can sleep on the ground. I don't want to take your bed, Adalaide," Sarah offered, then was mortified when she realized that they were probably used to sharing a sleeping place.

"Sarah, you've been ill for days. You shouldn't be sleeping on the ground, you could get sick again. You need to gather your strength for tomorrow," Hillard admonished.

It made sense to Sarah, but she still felt some slight jealousy that the two of them would be laying side by side all night. The image of it was so strong in her mind that she almost didn't notice that Hillard had not stopped speaking.

"I've been thinking about that information that Adalaide got at the castle. It really makes no sense to me for Lord Radek to be leaving the castle to look for you in the daylight hours – when he is at his most vulnerable. It would make more sense for him to be out now, in the dark, when you are likely to be sleeping somewhere and he is at his top strength. I more than half think that he is either trying to send you a message that you are safe tonight, so that you are easier to catch unaware, or that he knows that we are planning to rescue Christine and is setting a trap for us tomorrow."

Sarah couldn't believe that she hadn't thought of that. Of course, she didn't have as much experience in this world as the other two, but she thought of herself as someone who was at least decently intelligent. It seemed so obvious.

"Then what do we do now?" she asked in frustration.

"Well, I think we've already done it. We've taken you somewhere for the night where he won't find you. This place is sufficiently hidden so that he could walk down the path right above us and not see it. And vampires are not all-powerful. They *do* have an increased sense of smell, but they aren't tracking dogs. We have the rich earth all around us, insulating against our smell. We should be safe here until tomorrow." Hillard explained.

"And tomorrow? If he's expecting us then we can't just go in to get Christine." Sarah felt extreme frustration and helplessness. She just wanted to see her sister again.

"Oh, we are still going in tomorrow. We know he's expecting us. That will give us the upper hand. We just have to make sure we do things in a way that he isn't expecting." Hillard looked thoughtful. "Get some rest, Sarah. I'll think about this and come up with a plan for tomorrow. Don't worry. I'm not going to let him keep your sister. I think Lord Radek's reign of terror over this area is almost finished."

Sarah felt some measure of comfort at Hillard's determined expression, but she couldn't help but worry. There was still that knot in her stomach that had been there since they had first driven through the fog. She wondered if her life would ever be normal again. What *was* normal anyway? She'd just discovered that her husband was cheating on her. Sarah wondered what Paul was thinking about her disappearance. Was he missing her, or was he relieved that he hadn't had to face her? A single tear rolled down Sarah's cheek as feelings of helplessness and worthlessness washed over her. With her thoughts running in negative circles through her brain, she finally fell asleep.

# CHAPTER 11

After she was sure that Gervis was safely away, Christine walked over to her bed and sat down on the edge. Waves of exhaustion rolled over her body and she decided that it would be best if she got as much rest as possible before her escape attempt tomorrow. With any luck, she and Gervis would escape, and Lord Radek would be unsuccessful in his hunt for her sister. Then she could reunite with Sarah and they could flee to somewhere far away and out of Lord Radek's reach. She drifted off into sleep with the thought of finally reuniting with her sister comforting her.

When she awoke, it was dark, and she could sense that she wasn't alone. She sat up in her bed and found Lord Radek, sitting at the dressing table, watching her. She sat in the bed, frozen. She didn't know if she should say something or scream. The last time she had seen him he'd been drinking blood from her neck.

"Relax, Christine. I am not here to harm you." Lord Radek sounded tired, almost resigned.

"So, you aren't here to drink my blood?" Christine could feel hysteria rising within her. This man – vampire – struck waves of terror in her whenever she looked at him. At least until he somehow made her drop her defences and changed her feelings. At least that false sense of security he implanted in her never seemed to last. He couldn't seem to retain his control of her when she wasn't in his presence. She waited for that false sense of security to overwhelm her once again and was confused when it didn't.

"No. And if you promise to just talk with me, I will promise to never drink from you again."

Christine was shocked at this turn of events. What could have happened to change his behaviour in such a drastic way? "Why?" she asked bluntly.

"Because I cannot stop thinking about you. You have to know that you are different from any other fog traveller that has ever come through Donner. Normally, they are kept in the dungeons. I am sure you have sensed that Giselle does not approve of the unusual way I have been treating you."

Christine was really confused now. "I don't even know how I got here. I don't know *how* you treat other people. But I'm sure that if you treat them even worse than you treat me, you probably don't have a lot of friends." Part of her was afraid that he would be offended at her words, and part of her was happy to be able to speak her mind without her emotions being tampered with.

Lord Radek looked down at the floor. "You are right. I do not have a lot of friends. None, actually.  I have not had a real friend for over five hundred years. But you remind me of someone from my childhood – someone who was very special to me. You remind me what it was like to have someone to talk to, to share things with."

"Five hundred years?" She knew that vampires were supposed to be immortal, but he looked like he was no more than thirty years old.

"You know what I am. I have seen the recognition in your eyes. Do you have vampires in your world?"

"Only in stories. They aren't real. At least not where I come from."

"Well, in this world we are real. And we have ruled this world for over five hundred years. We take care of the human populations under us, and in return, they give us the gift of their blood."

"I haven't *given* you anything!" Christine blurted at him. "You've taken it from me. I don't call that a gift – that's stealing! It's like rape!"

Lord Radek seemed to shrink within himself a bit as she shouted at him. Then a small smile crossed his face as he looked back up at her. "Normally, I would never let anyone speak to me like that. They would not dare. I would drain them on the spot and they would never speak again. When you speak to me like that, however, I feel ashamed. You look so very much like her. She would be horrified to see what I have become."

"Who?" asked Christine, puzzled at this strange change in demeanour.

"My sister. Her name was Anja. Her hair was golden like yours and her eyes shone with the same fire. Your faces are not the same, but she had the same way of holding her chin straight out when she was angry and so very many of your mannerism remind me of her. I thought I had forgotten her, that she was one of the things from my past that had slipped into non-existence, like so many other things have, but you brought her back to me."

"Was she a vampire too?" Christine was curious now, about this person who, just by a simple resemblance to her, had caused this change in Lord Radek.

"No, I never had the chance. She died when she was only sixteen and I was fourteen. I was not turned until I was twenty-three. Even then, it was forbidden to make another vampire without permission, but I think that if Anja had been alive, I would have done it anyway, I loved her so much."

Christine was astonished by this turn of events. This monster was showing an all-too-human side of himself. She was very curious about his story, and the story of how this world came to be so different from her own.

"I've got many questions about this world," she said, hesitantly, wondering if he would answer her, or if the sound of her voice would break this apparent reverie and bring back the monster she was accustomed to seeing in him.

"I know. I have never spoken to a fog traveller before like this." He chuckled wryly. "I have not spoken to anyone like this for so long. I think we have many things to talk about."

"Were you serious when you said you wouldn't drink from me again?" she asked, almost afraid to hear the truth.

"Yes. I cannot do it, especially after you told me that it felt like rape. I could not do it to her, and I find myself no longer wanting to drink from you."

Christine was flabbergasted. This was the last thing she had expected to happen. Then, another thought crossed her mind. "But what about my sister – I thought you were going to find her tomorrow? Are you planning to drink from her instead?"

Lord Radek looked confused and suspicious for a moment and Christine realized that she had put Gervis in danger by revealing what she knew about Lord Radek's plans. He quickly recovered and said, "I am going to find her for you. I do not know much about this vampire she is with. He is a renegade, and I should have taken care of him a long time ago. I am going to find her to bring her here to keep you company and to keep her safe. I will promise to never drink from her if you want."

Christine looked at him. Was he telling the truth? To protect Gervis, she said, "I heard two people talking in the hall about it. I was worried that you were going to be drinking from both of us."

He looked into her eyes. "Christine, it is my right as the Vampire Lord of these parts to drink from any fog traveller that arrives. But I promise you, if you stay with me, I will keep you and your sister safe."

"You keep saying that about the fog travellers. How did we get here? What causes the fog?"

Lord Radek sighed. "When the vampires first came to be, we were a reckless race. We were drunk on our power and our thirst for blood. The humans could not resist us and their numbers shrunk very rapidly. Conflict started to grow between groups of vampires as the numbers of our food source shrank. There was a great battle and, in order to regain our strength, the humans were fed on even more. It was at this time that the fogs first arrived. No one knows exactly what caused it, but some say that it was a great vampire prophet, who saw us as a beautiful race and saw that we had potential for greatness, if we did not destroy ourselves first. Humans started coming through the fogs, which appeared around the world at specific locations once a month. With our food supply rejuvenated the conflict died down and a form of global government was formed. Close to each fog gate, a settlement was created. A vampire was put in charge of each settlement to rule as they see fit. They are bound by only one rule – no other vampires can be made without permission of the Vampire Council. So we each have our place where we are as gods to our human subjects, but solitary in our existence."

Christine was having a hard time processing all of the new information. This world was so very different from her own. "So you only feed from the fog travellers?"

Lord Radek chuckled. "No. That is like suggesting that you could only eat from one chicken for a month. A vampire requires more sustenance. In return for my protection and rulership, my subjects each give me a gift of blood one or more times a year. It has become our way of life, our whole economic system is based on the Geshenk – the gift of life."

Christine didn't know how to feel about this information. It was all so different from the way of life she knew. "Don't the humans hate it?"

Lord Radek looked surprised at the question. "No. It is the way things are. It may seem very different from the world you knew, but for them it is the way things have always been. They benefit from the situation too, however. Do people still die from disease in your world?"

Christine thought about the AIDS epidemic, the SARS scare from a few years ago, and the random outbreaks of Ebola in the African regions. There was Bird Flu outbreaks and Mad Cow Disease all over the world as well. "Yes. We have found cures for many of the old diseases through science, but more show up all the time."

"Disease is no longer the threat it once was to the human populations. A few tiny drops of a vampire's blood on their tongue, or mixed with their food, kills any disease that is attacking their body. Wounds that would once have been fatal are healed in much the same way."

Christine was amazed. "People must live for a very long time then!"

"They live until their late fifties sometimes. Things are much better than they once were."

Christine was surprised at the age he had provided. People in her world lived to an average age of seventy five, and some even made it past one hundred. If there was no more disease, what caused them to die so young? Then she remembered the Geschenk that Lord Radek had mentioned. Constant blood loss must weaken their bodies in some way that caused them to die younger in this world.  She was not going to tell Lord Radek that though, at least not at this time.

"So, if you aren't going to feed on me anymore, what do you want me for?"

"I want to have someone to talk to – to share my thoughts with. I have been alone for such a very long time. I want to know what it feels like again to have someone to share my thoughts with."

"But I want to go home to my own world. I have a life there. I'm a teacher. There are children there who will miss me."

"Christine, there is no way for you to get back. I do not even know if the gate works in both directions. But what I do know is that it is a different world each time. The people who come through are very similar in many ways, but those I have interrogated have always described a world with some difference, small as it may be."

"I don't understand. There are more worlds?" Christine was still feeling sleepy and was having a difficult time wrapping her mind around all of the information she was receiving in such a short time.  "Are they different planets? Or are they all just different versions of Earth?"

"I do not completely understand it either. I do believe that it is the same planet. You did not come from some far away star. There are too many similarities to ignore that fact. You do recognise the land mass across the big water, do you not?"

Christine smiled unexpectedly.  "Yes, it's the same view I have from my kitchen at home."

"Well, I have never met a fog traveller who came through here who did not recognise it. Other things may change, but the land remains the same."

"So I'll never see my kitchen again? I'll never see my class again? What will they think happened to me? I just disappeared. They might think I was kidnapped, or murdered."

"I know it is difficult to accept, Christine. Your life has changed drastically in the last few days. I am afraid I have made things even more difficult for you, although I now regret my actions. I am going to leave you now so that you can get some rest. I just want you to know that you can stay here as long as you like, and when we find your sister, she is welcome here as well. I promise to take care of the both of you and to never drink from you as long as you promise to stay, in the name of friendship."

Christine didn't know how to answer him. She felt like he deserved some response, but she wasn't sure if she could trust him. He seemed genuine enough, but he'd given her no reason in the past to believe him now. She said nothing.

Lord Radek waited for a moment, and then seemed to accept that she would give him no response. He rose from his place at the dressing table and walked over to the bed. He lifted her hand from the covers where it was resting and raised it to his lips. Christine winced, expecting to feel his teeth sink into her flesh and was shocked when he simply kissed her hand, looked deeply into her eyes for a moment, and walked quietly out of the room.

Christine lay back down in the bed and just let the thoughts whirl tumultuously in her brain. She didn't know how to make sense of everything right now. After only a few minutes, it seemed that her brain gave up, and she fell asleep.

Sarah woke up to someone gently shaking her shoulder. She opened her eyes and for a moment was startled by the dirt walls that surrounded her.

"What time is it?" she asked groggily. She couldn't tell if it was day or night because they were still underground.

"It's just before dawn," answered Hillard, taking his hand off her shoulder. "We're going to get an early start, and hopefully Lord Radek will not be expecting us until later in the day."

It sounded like a reasonable idea to Sarah. Not that she truly understood why they were still going in during the day, when it seemed like Lord Radek wouldn't be out of the castle after all. Maybe it was because that was when he would be at his weakest – inside the castle or out. As long as they got her sister out, she really didn't care what time of day they left.

They quickly packed up, bringing only a very small amount of food and water for the short hike to the castle, and some weapons. Hillard took only a small knife from the wall. Adalaide took a sword. Sarah looked at them both questioningly. She didn't know how to use a weapon. She'd never used a knife for anything more serious than cutting food.

"Don't worry. Here, just take this knife. Use it only if you have to. I know you probably have no combat experience." Hillard smiled at her reassuringly as he handed her a small knife, similar to the one he tucked in his own belt.

"That's an understatement. I've never hurt anyone in my life. I don't even know if I could use this if my life depended on it."

Adalaide smiled grimly. "You would be surprised at what you can do when your life depends on it."

They began their trek through the woods, towards the castle. They'd only been travelling for a short time when Hillard stopped to pick up a thick branch from the ground. As they continued walking, he carved the end into a sharp point with the knife he had taken from the wall. Once he was finished, he placed the stake in his bag and found another stick to sharpen. By the time they were within sight of the castle, just a couple of hours later, he had five such sticks in his pack. When he spotted the turrets of the castle he motioned for the small group to stop.

"Okay, Sarah. Here's my plan. I need you to have courage. You want to get your sister back, right?"

"I wouldn't be here if I didn't," she answered, annoyed that he had even asked.

"I'll be taking you into the castle. I'm going to say that I found you and that I want a reward from Lord Radek for bringing you to him."

"What?!" Sarah was shocked. "*This* is your plan? You'll be turning me in to Lord Radek?"

"Hear me out. You admit that you have no experience in combat. You aren't going to be at your most useful if we go into the castle fighting our way in. However, if I bring you in, they will more than likely bring you to Christine. Adalaide, in the mean time, will be sneaking in through the kitchens, using her in-castle contacts to help her out. I'll keep Lord Radek occupied while she goes up to the room where your sister, and most likely you, will be staying. She'll pick the lock, get the two of you out and by the time Lord Radek has kicked me out, you will both already be free." Hillard stared intently at Adalaide as he spoke. It seemed as if she wanted to ask him a question, but didn't want to say anything in front of Sarah. Finally, Hillard just nodded at her and Adalaide seemed satisfied.

Sarah tried to just ignore the silent communication between the two. She was sure that Adalaide was worried that her lover might get hurt or even killed by Lord Radek. Sarah was concerned about him too, but tried not to think about it. All she should be thinking about at this point was rescuing Christine.

Adalaide gave Sarah a brief, strong hug and whispered in her ear, "I will see you soon. Be ready." And then she was off into the woods, presumably towards the castle kitchens.

Hillard took Sarah's hand in his for a moment. His emerald eyes stared into hers and he looked unsure of what to say. Sarah was confused for a moment, because there seemed to be so many emotions crossing his face at once.

"I can do this," she asserted, trying to be brave. "You don't have to worry about me."

"I've been worrying about you almost from the moment we met, Sarah." He squeezed her hand tightly. "I'm afraid of what may happen in there, just like you are. I believe in what we are doing. You need to be with your sister." He almost sounded like he was trying to convince himself of something. "You don't need me." He sighed.

Now Sarah was really confused. He sounded almost as if he cared more about her than as just a friend. She decided to take a chance.

"I do need you, Hillard. This world is so different from mine. But you're different too. You're different from any man I have ever met before. I've half convinced myself that all of this is just a dream, but if I knew for a fact that at least you were real, I think I could accept it."

Hillard looked at her for a moment. He was thinking that even if he were successful today, he would likely be killed in his efforts to get this special woman back together with her sister. One kiss couldn't hurt.

He grasped her to him tightly, hugging her against his body. A kiss could be a terrible thing. If he were killed, she would be devastated. If he were not, there could be no future between them.

"I *am* real, Sarah. And I promise to keep you safe." It was the best he could offer her. He knew from the expression in her eyes that she was disappointed and confused, but he didn't know how to fix things. There was no cure for his curse and he could never make another of his kind.

Hillard took Sarah's hand and lead her towards the castle.

# Chapter 12

Christine awoke just as the sun was coming over the horizon. Remembering her late night conversation with Lord Radek the evening before, she felt conflicted and confused as to what to do now. She knew that Gervis would be arriving soon to help her to escape from the castle. But, if Lord Radek had been telling her the truth last night, that might be exactly the wrong thing to do. Hearing him talk like that made him seem to be a very sympathetic person. It must have been horrible living centuries alone, without a single confidant to share experiences and thoughts with. If she and Sarah truly were trapped in this world, life could be worse than living in a castle. She heard a noise from behind her bedroom wall and the secret door swung open.

Despite her conflicting thoughts, a radiant smile spread across Christine's face when she saw Gervis peeking into her room. She rushed over and hugged him. Then she held him out at arm's length to inspect him. He looked slightly pale, but otherwise healthy. He seemed to have recovered from his punishment after his last visit to her.

"Gervis, I don't know if I can go today." Christine quickly explained about her late night visit from Lord Radek and the things that he had revealed to her.

Gervis looked thoughtful. "I've never heard him to speak so to anyone before. Lord Radek is the lord of this area. He has never chosen to be so open with anyone before. But, I have to tell you, Christine, that things here in Donner aren't as he made them out to be."

"What do you mean?"

"If a person gets sick, he charges their family or loved ones a full Geschenk to heal them. If there is no one to pay, he then drains the person – to put them out of their misery, he says. People don't live as long in Donner as they do in the other settlements, because Lord Radek is so harsh with his pricing and his penalties. The slightest crime is punished by death – even a simple fist fight results in the death of both parties, no matter who is to blame. No, Christine, I think it's amazing that he opened up to you as he did, but he wasn't honest with you. He isn't known for his truthful ways."

Christine thought for a moment. She wanted to believe in the Lord Radek that she had seen last night. "Maybe he's just like that because he's been alone so long. Maybe I could help to change things around here."

Gervis looked hurt at Christine's insistence on defending Lord Radek. "Oh, he can be a charmer, all right. But are you willing to risk the life of your sister on the word of someone who has drunk of your blood, and who nearly killed me for merely speaking to you?"

That took Christine aback. She wanted to see the best in everyone, but Gervis was right. Her sister's life depended on her making the right choices right now.

"Where's Lord Radek right now? Has he left yet?" she asked, slowly building up the confidence she would need to make the escape attempt.

"He's here in the castle, but he's asleep. He spent the night looking for your sister instead of going today. This works better for us, because he's less likely to wake from his deep sleep than for us to have encountered him on the outside after escaping if he had really been out looking for your sister today."

That made sense to Christine. She took Gervis' hand in her own and looked into his warm chocolaty eyes. "Thank you for this, Gervis." She gave him a brief kiss on the cheek and then smiled as she saw the blush creeping across his face. He was so sweet and childlike in some ways. She wondered how long he had been living in the castle.

Gervis shook his head, almost as if to clear it, then led Christine out the secret door and into a musty old tunnel. The tunnel was shorter than she had expected, and when they emerged, it was into a bedroom even more enormous and extravagant than her own.

"Whose room is this?" she asked in awe.

"Lord Radek's" Gervis replied shortly, pulling her quickly through the door to the room and out into the hall.

"But I thought you said he was in bed.  There was no one in there."

"He doesn't sleep there," Gervis replied tightly. "You need to be quiet. I don't want anyone to catch us."

"Oh, but someone has," came a throaty voice from behind them.

Christine and Gervis both turned quickly and gasped in unison. Lord Radek had been waiting for them in the hall!

"Are you going somewhere Christine? I have been waiting for you to come out of your room and come down for breakfast. You did not have to take that route out of your room – I left your door unlocked when I left last night."

Christine's eyes widened. She could have escaped at any time in the night. He had actually trusted her to stay after their talk and now he had caught her trying to escape. She saw his emerald eyes sparkle dangerously as he came closer to her.

"All I wanted was for you to stay. I might even have kept my promise to never feed on you again. I would even have spared Gervis. But now, I must punish you!" Lord Radek's mouth burrowed into Christine's neck and this time, instead of pleasure, she felt only terror and the pain of the tear in her skin. She could feel the blood pouring out of the open wound in her neck and into Lord Radek's mouth. Weakness buckled her legs and, with surprising strength, Radek held her up as he drank. Christine felt her consciousness slipping away, but was forced back into wakefulness by a new wave of terror flowing through her entire body. The terror could not withstand the weakness that began to envelope her, however, and she knew that she was very near death.

Even the terror was not enough to keep her tied to this earth. As she felt herself slipping away, she felt something other than terror – a sense of regret and desperation and heard a faint cry from the lips of Lord Radek.

"Damn you Christine! What have you done to me? I did not want this for you. I do not *want* to let you go. I must have you here with me!"

Christine felt a few drops of moisture touch her lips. Weakly, her tongue touched the moisture and she felt an immediate surge of strength return to her body. Soon, fluid was rushing through her lips and down her throat, and she was drinking it greedily. She was *so very* thirsty. She felt as if Lord Radek had drained every ounce of moisture from her body and she now had such a deep aching thirst.

Finally, after what felt like an eternity, she opened her eyes. She was lying on the floor and Lord Radek was kneeling beside her. What stood out to her most of all, however, was the sight of Gervis, staring at her in utter horror.

"I'm okay Gervis. I'm better now. I'm just really thirsty. Could you get me something to drink?" she gasped.

If possible, Gervis' look of horror only increased and Christine heard Lord Radek chuckle. "That is exactly what I was thinking. Gervis, do be so kind as to give your lady a drink."

A new look came over Gervis now. His eyes were full of admiration and worship for Christine. He approached her with a sense of reverence and as he kneeled before her, he turned to Lord Radek and murmured, "but I have no cup to fill for her."

Lord Radek chuckled his ominous chuckle again. "There is no need for a chalice my boy. You want her, do you not?" Gervis nodded. "Then let her drink from you."

Gervis pressed his wrist against Christine's mouth and she was suddenly horrified as the true meaning of Lord Radek's words became clear to her. Before she could protest, however, the thirst within her became too overwhelming and she found her mouth moving of its own accord and latching itself to Gervis' wrist. The first burst of human blood between her lips was a shock. It was more delicious than the finest wine she had ever drunk. She couldn't get enough of it. As she drank, she could feel not only Gervis' skin touching her lips, but the feeling of deep satisfaction that he had. She could feel that he liked her and wanted to be with her. She could feel that with the slightest effort, she could make him love her.

Slowly, the emotions she was feeling from him were starting to fade. A sense of disappointment grew within her until she realized that he was weakening under her grasp.

"NO!" she shouted, as she realized that she was killing him. As she leapt back from Gervis, he slumped to the floor. She started to go to him, but the closer she got to him, the more her thirst seemed to grow for him.

"Is he still alive?" she asked, her voice trembling.

Lord Radek reached down for Gervis' wrist, placed a drop of his own blood on the wound and replied, "Yes, but barely. I am surprised that you had the self-control to stop. I did not when I was first sired."

Slowly, realization was beginning to dawn. Christine looked down at herself. She didn't look any different than she usually did, but she felt so much stronger, so much more alive. How could this be possible? A few days ago, vampires were just a fairy tale. Now could it be possible that she had become one? How could she ever face Sarah again?!

Sarah followed Hillard obediently into the castle. They had agreed that Sarah would play the part of a concerned sister and Hillard the part of the rescuer who wanted a reward for his troubles. Hillard had expected more resistance from the castle guards, but they just waved the two of them in, almost as if they had been expected. Hillard hoped that it was more that they were just not expecting trouble. He wasn't counting on it though.

At the front doors, a kindly looking woman opened the door as they approached. "Well, you must be Lady Christine's sister," she said, looking a little disconcerted as she said Christine's name. "Lord Radek is expecting you."

This was not what they had been hoping for. They had hoped that he would be caught at least a little bit off guard by their appearance and now it seemed that they were falling into a trap after all. Stoically, they entered the house, where they were lead down a grand hallway and into a large room. Unbeknownst to them, this was the same room in which Christine had first met Lord Radek.

Lord Radek was standing in much the same place as he had when he had first met Christine. This time, however, as the two entered the room, they were surrounded by guards, who quickly removed the pack from Hillard. They didn't search Sarah, however, which she found a little insulting – almost as if she couldn't possibly be dangerous – but she was relieved that she still had the small knife, even though she knew she couldn't hurt Lord Radek with it. She looked up at him defiantly and was struck by the shocking emerald hue of his eyes, so similar to that of Hillard's beautiful eyes. It was such a rare colouring that she wondered if the two of them were related somehow. Of course, that couldn't be true – Lord Radek was hundreds of years old and Hillard couldn't be more than thirty.

"You must be Sarah," Lord Radek said, his voice echoing in the great room, "I have to say, I am surprised that you do not look more like your sister. She is quite beautiful."

Sarah felt as if she had been slapped by his words. She knew that she wasn't as pretty as her sister, but it was ridiculous that this monster felt that he had the right to judge her appearance. "Where is my sister? Is she okay? If you've hurt her …" Sarah finished her rant there, not knowing how to threaten someone who so obviously could overpower her with no effort at all.

Lord Radek chuckled. "It seems that you are as feisty as your sister. She is fine. Christine is upstairs in her room. Giselle will take you to her if you like." The kindly woman stepped into the room and nodded her head. Lord Radek continued, "Hillard and I have some matters that require discussion. Some things, I am afraid, that are long overdue."

Sarah did not like the sound of that last bit, especially since the guards had taken Hillard's bag from him, containing the wooden stakes and flint for fire, but she had no choice but to follow Giselle. Her part of this plan was only beginning. Now it was Hillard's job to keep Lord Radek busy while she and Adalaide got Christine out of the castle.

Sarah paid careful attention as she was lead through the halls of the castle. She wanted to make sure that she could find her way back out again after she was reunited with Christine. They went up one floor and finally stopped in front of a heavy wooden door.

"This is her room. You can go in. I think she's expecting you," Giselle said warily and then turned, leaving Sarah standing alone in front of the door. Sarah didn't know what to do next so she knocked, feeling foolish knocking on a door in a rescue attempt. Something didn't seem quite right here.

"Come in," Christine's voice came through the door. Sarah was so excited to hear her sister's voice that she rushed into the room without thinking any further about her suspicions. Christine was standing in front of the door and the first thing Sarah did was rush over and envelop her in a hug.

"Are you okay? Has he hurt you? We're going to get you out of here." Sarah knew she was babbling but she had been so afraid that she would never see Christine again that she couldn't help it. She held Christine out at arm's length and was shocked at what she saw.

Christine's beautiful blue eyes were now the shocking emerald hue shared by both Radek and Hillard!

# CHAPTER 13

Lord Radek and Hillard stood across the room from each other after Sarah left, watching each other like wary dogs before a fight.

"So, you are the renegade," began Lord Radek. "I have sensed your presence here in my lands now for the past ten or fifteen years. I have wondered what exactly it was you were doing here. I know that it is my job to destroy anyone not sanctioned by the Vampire Council, but you have intrigued me. You do not feed on any of my subjects – not that I am aware of anyway. Are you so pathetic that you feed on the dumb blood of animals?"

"If I choose not to kill my own kind to quench my thirst, I would say that it's no business of yours," asserted Hillard calmly. He hadn't been sure of what this confrontation with Lord Radek would bring, but this was definitely an interesting beginning.

"But they are *not* your own kind, Hillard. Surely you know that. You are above them now. Like a god. Who was it that made you?

Who left you so unaware of your place in life?" Lord Radek was curious as to what vampire would not only go against the Vampire Council in making another without permission, but also leave that new vampire alone and unaware of his rightful place in the world.

"Cedrik of Zwischenmeer. I know you know who *he* was."

"Ah, my old whelp. He was my great mistake. Do you know *why* he made you?" Lord Radek was truly curious. He was unaware that Cedrik had had the courage to do anything except take his own life.

"Yes." Hillard was curious as to where this was going. How could Lord Radek be aware of him all this time and not know of his true intention in coming to Donner?

"You seem so hostile. I know that there are things to be settled between us. Perhaps *that* is why Cedrik made you. But it has been so long since I have been in the company of one of my own kind. This has been a most interesting day. Come, sit my boy, allow me to share my Geschenk with you. Let us exchange stories before we get down to business. It is always good to know your enemy. Perhaps we could become friends, or even allies. This day has changed my plans for the future, and I am still waiting to see how things will turn out." Lord Radek sat on one of the couches and indicated that Hillard should take a seat in the adjacent one.

Hillard was now even more curious as to where this was going than before. He had no intention of becoming Lord Radek's friend, let alone his ally, but it was said that you should know your enemy, and he was curious to see how much more he could learn of his own kind before he had to deal with Lord Radek. Plus, the longer he kept Radek talking, the more time Sarah and Christine would have to escape.

Sarah stared into Christine's eyes with horror. What did it mean? Christine saw the look in Sarah's eyes and knew that her sister saw the difference in her.

"What is it Sarah?" she asked softly, afraid to hear the answer.

"Your eyes.  They're green – so *very* green. What did he do to you Chris?"

Christine felt the thirst throbbing within her. It had begun even before Sarah had entered the room. She was resisting the urge to drink from her sister with every single ounce of her being. It was bad enough that Sarah could see that she was changed – there was no way that she would ever drink from her. Inwardly, Christine was in despair.  How could she continue to live, knowing that she might accidentally take a life, like she had almost done with Gervis only a few hours before? How could she ever walk among humans again, feeling this irresistible urge to feed upon them? How could she go with her sister now, when Sarah's unselfish act of rescuing her could end in her death?

When Christine didn't answer, Sarah became deeply afraid for her sister. Was this even her sister? If they were in a parallel world, it was possible for this to be an impostor.

"It's me Sarah." Christine had sensed her sister's suspicion and knew the thoughts that were coming with it, even if she couldn't read them directly. "I'm okay. But I'm not the same. I don't think I can go with you." Seeing Sarah's look of despair, she continued. "I *want* to go with you. I really do. But I can't trust myself. This feeling, this urge, it's just too strong. I never want to hurt you."

Sarah looked at her sister in horror. "He made you like him," she gasped in realization. She just stared at Christine for a moment. "How? Why?"

Christine smiled a wistful half smile. "I tried to escape this morning. He caught us. He was so very angry. I think that he almost killed me. But at the last moment he stopped. He isn't a total monster, Sarah. There's something about him that is so very lonely. We have become … friends … almost. But I betrayed that when I tried to escape and, in his anger, Lord Radek almost drained me. I think at the last moment he regretted it, because that's when he did this to me. He saved me, Sarah, but I think he cursed me at the same time."

"Not a total monster?" Sarah couldn't believe that she had heard those words coming out of her sister's mouth. "He drank your blood! He's a vampire! Of course he's a monster!"

Christine looked at her sister. "Am I a monster then too, Sarah?"

"You haven't drunk anyone's blood!" Sarah protested, realizing her mistake. Christine was just Christine. She wasn't a monster, she was her sister.

Christine looked down at the floor. Tears welled to her eyes. "I have though, Sarah – the man who was escaping with me, Gervis. I almost killed him."

"You drank from someone? You actually drank his blood?" Sarah backed away from Christine in horror. She almost fled from the room, but then she saw Christine's face. There was a look of utter despair painted across it. There were tears in her eyes. It was obvious that this was still her sister. "Why did you do it?" Sarah asked, needing to hear a logical answer for it all.

"I couldn't help myself. The thirst – you wouldn't understand how powerful it is. Even now, I can almost smell your blood. But Sarah, I will *never* drink from you. I'll die before I ever hurt you, or anyone, ever again. I'll kill myself. I *want* to die. I think it would have been better if Lord Radek had just let me die. I wouldn't have to worry about hurting other people and I wouldn't have to see that look of disgust and horror that's on your face when you look at me."

Sarah tried to stifle the fear of her sister that she felt. This was still her sister. They had been through so much together that she couldn't imagine her life without Christine. She needed to find some way to help her sister.

"Maybe Hillard knows a way to help you. Maybe not all vampires are evil. Maybe you can drink just enough to survive and not actually hurt anyone."

Christine started at hearing Hillard's name. "Is Hillard the vampire you were with? Is he as bad as Lord Radek said? He said that Hillard was a rogue – whatever that means."

Sarah just stared at Christine, unable to believe what she had just heard. Hillard? A vampire? Suddenly, the significance of the emerald green eyes struck her. She felt as if she had been punched in the stomach.

"You didn't know." It was more of a statement coming from Christine's mouth than a question. It was obvious when she looked at Sarah that she was shocked and even more horrified than before.

Christine hoped that Sarah would be able to handle all of these shocks coming at her.

"No." Sarah wanted to say more, but didn't know what to say. She felt horribly betrayed by Hillard. He hadn't tried to drink from her, but knowing that she had been alone with him so much, and even unconscious in his presence, made her wonder if he really had drunk from her without her realizing it. And the feelings she had been developing for him — were they real? Or were they simply projections from him? Were the things that he had told her about vampires true? She had no idea what to think anymore. She just knew that her sister was standing in front of her, afraid that she would be left alone.

There was a knock on the door and Sarah grabbed Christine's hand. "We'll figure out what to do together. That's what we always do. I'll help you in any way I can."

"But what if I hurt you? Maybe I'm better off staying here with Lord Radek."

"NO!" Sarah voice was emphatic. "I am *not* leaving you here with him. You are my sister — you won't hurt me. I trust in you. Now *you* need to trust in me."

Sarah led Christine to the door and opened it. Adalaide stood in the hallway, with Giselle and a man. "Gervis" she heard Christine whisper softly behind her. She knew from the man's pale countenance and the fact that he was being held up by both Adalaide and Giselle that this must be the man her sister had fed on.

"Giselle made me promise to take Gervis with us when we leave. She is afraid that Lord Radek will kill him," Adalaide said by way of an explanation. Her eyes widened as she noticed the colour of Christine's own shining orbs.

"You take him to his parents! Don't let *her* be alone with him! I'm holding you two responsible for him. Don't let her cause him any more trouble!" Giselle snapped, her face white with anger.

Sarah didn't know what to say, so she just took Gervis' arm from Giselle and started helping him down the hall. Christine was quiet and subdued as she followed. Giselle led the way down through the servant's area and out through the kitchen.

Before they left, Giselle threw out one more, "You keep him safe, Adalaide. Don't let that vampire witch alone near him. I'm holding you responsible!" Then she slammed the kitchen door after them and they were moving as fast as they could towards the woods and Adalaide's hideaway.

"Let me first tell you my story, then I would like to hear yours." Lord Radek picked up a small bell from the table beside him. He rang it and a petite young girl came into the room carrying a tray with two glasses of red liquid on it. Hillard stared at the glasses. He had rarely partaken of human blood in the past and always found it difficult to go back to drinking animal blood afterwards. He would have refused outright if he was not afraid of enraging Lord Radek and putting the plan to rescue Christine in danger. He sipped the blood sparingly, trying to ignore the instinctual need within him to gulp it down. He had fed on animal blood the night before, slipping away from the hideout after Sarah had fallen asleep, so his need for nourishment was not great, but the temptation of real human blood was great within him and his thirst was raging.

Lord Radek seemed to notice Hillard's discomfort. "Drink as much as you like. I have a copious supply and do not mind sharing with you today, if you will grant me the pleasure of your company for a short while."

At that, something within Hillard snapped, and he downed the blood in one gulp, feeling deeply ashamed immediately afterwards for his lack of self-control. He tried to comfort himself with the fact that, by drinking, he was increasing his strength so that he would be at his strongest when he had to finally face Lord Radek in battle.

Lord Radek rang the bell twice, and the young girl re-entered the room, her tray holding three bottles of dark liquid. She placed the tray on the table and left again, never saying a word.

"She is very pretty, is she not?" mused Lord Radek, "Her father died before she was born, and her mother died when she was three. I took her into my own house when there was no one in the village willing to take her in. Despite what you may think of me, I try to take care of those under my responsibility."

Hillard said nothing. He thought that it was more likely that the girl's parents had been killed by Lord Radek, but knew better than to say so out loud.

Watching Hillard for a moment, Radek finally cleared his throat. "Well, now. I was born in the year 1512, in a small village in Germany. I remember when Charles came into power. I was just a young man when I joined his army. I rose quickly through the ranks, distinguishing myself in battle. I was alone in the world, you see, and the army became my family."

"I was turned by Charles himself in 1535. We had no special bond, he and I, but I was one of his greatest human soldiers, and became one of his best vampire warriors. Those days were filled with blood. I remember drinking my fill and then some at every battle. It was a glorious time for the vampire!"

"When the Vampire Council came into power, those times ended. It was obvious that if we kept killing humans at such a high rate we would soon deplete our food supply. Many of the members of the Council felt threatened by my battle prowess and I was banished to the New World, where I established the settlement of Donner."

Hillard nodded. He doubted the part about the Vampire Council feeling threatened by Lord Radek, but the rest of the history was familiar to him. Cedrik had told him some of Lord Radek's history, before succumbing to the fires, and the rest he had read in the libraries of Cedrik's castle, before heading out towards Donner.

"As to your sire," Lord Radek continued, "I was given permission to create a new vampire when the Lord Vampire of the neighbouring land, Zwischenmeer, was killed by the rioting of his own subjects. The Council was mortified that one of their own could be so weak, and they wanted me to make a point of filling the position quickly. Cedrik was the captain of my guards at the time. I never thought to ask him if he wanted to serve as a Vampire Lord, I simply thought it was such a great honour that he would be eager for the chance to serve. I also saw the opportunity there to increase my own power in the area. Cedrik would look to me for guidance, or so I thought."

"But I had never considered Cedrik's past. I had been responsible for the deaths of both his parents.  He hated the vampiric gift and all that it represented. I put him in place in Zwischenmeer and it all fell apart. In a village where the subjects were already angry, Cedrik was far out of his league. He knew how to use his emotional influence, so the villagers could not get too close to him. But, the first time one did get close, his hunger overtook him and he killed, not one, but several villagers. I believe it was the foolish guilt he felt over their deaths that pushed him over the edge."

Hillard nodded again. Cedrik had told him much of that. In fact, it had been Cedrik who had told him that it was possible to survive on animal blood alone. In the weeks where he had been too afraid to leave the castle, and not able to bring himself to request the Geschenk, he had been sneaking out of the castle at night, draining any animals he could find in the forest. It was not the same as human blood – much in the same way that wild game tasted different from a cow raised on grass and feed, animal blood tasted wild and was not as satisfying to the palate.

"Now, tell me of the end of Cedrik," Lord Radek insisted. "And tell me of how you came to be here. I do believe we can be of some use to each other. There is no need for us to be enemies."

Hillard paused for a moment before beginning. It was strange how Lord Radek kept referring to the potential of friendship between them. It wasn't something he had been expecting.  He had hoped to be able to engage the Lord in some sort of dialogue before initiating battle with him, in the hopes of extending the amount of time that Sarah and Christine had to escape, but this was completely unexpected.

"Well," he began, uncertainly, "I suppose I should start at the beginning. When I was a boy, my parents lived in a small cottage on the outskirts of Zwischenmeer. I remember being very happy there. In my ninth year, a terrible illness came through our village. The Vampire Lord, Lord Cathal, healed as many as he could. However, by the time the other villagers noticed that my parents were missing and came to investigate, they were both dead, and I was very near death myself. They brought me to the castle and Lord Cathal not only healed me, but allowed me to stay in the castle, under the care of his servant, Gretchen, who probably filled a role very similar to your Giselle."

Lord Radek nodded and Hillard continued. "After the plague, the villagers became more and more unhappy with the rulership of Lord Cathal. He had charged his normal rate for healing during the time of the plague – one Geschenk – and afterwards, many of the villagers did not have enough Stück left to buy food. A time of great poverty hit Zwischenmeer then, although those of us who lived in the castle did not feel its effects. The villagers became so dissatisfied that a rebellion started – first quiet, and then it came out in the open. It began with villagers quietly beginning their own bartering system, disregarding the Geschenk system. It was the logical way for them to go when most of them had no Stück left with which to buy food. All they had was their services. The village really pulled together. But Lord Cathal noticed that his blood supply was getting low and began to punish the villagers for breaking the law. He took blood from the offenders against their will. The villagers had realized by this time, however, that they could survive without the system of Blood Economics. They needed someone to blame for the deaths of those who had succumbed to the plague and focused all of their energy and rage on Lord Cathal. The rebellion became more and more vocal then and, at the end, the villagers came together, destroyed the Blood Bank, and fled into the forest. Lord Cathal had been slowly becoming weaker as time progressed and his blood supply shrank. He went out into the forest one night to find the villagers and punish them, but was too weak by that time to focus his emotional powers on all of the villagers. He, unlike me, did not know that he could have kept up his strength by consuming the blood of animals. They overwhelmed him and set him ablaze. That was the end of Lord Cathal."

Hillard paused. "I had liked Lord Cathal. I had never experienced any of the things that had so angered the villagers, so I felt nothing but grief at his death. In all the time that he was suffering from hunger, while the villagers were withholding the Geschenk from him, he didn't take from any of his household staff. He could have – it would have saved him – but he was of the old vampires and believed that it was his right to have the Geschenk and he was outraged that any of the villagers would withhold it from him after he had served them and their ancestors for over two hundred years. I think it was the thirst that caused him to so badly misjudge the situation. A merchant group came through a few days after his death, and the people of Zwischenmeer had no Stück left to trade with. The merchants left,

I assume coming here, and the villagers began to realize that their situation was not as good as they had first considered. Without the Geschenk, they could trade with no one outside of their own village. Of course, some merchants might be willing to trade for goods, but they would fear reprisals from the other Vampire Lords if they got caught trading with a group of rebels like the people of Zwischenmeer. "

"Then, a few weeks later, you arrived with Cedrik. I'm sure you don't remember me, but I remember seeing you. I was the one who stabled your horses when you arrived. Cedrik seemed much more confident when he was in your presence than he did after you left. I performed most of the household chores for him. I was the only one who had stayed in the castle after the death of Lord Cathal, everyone else having family in the village. One or two of the servants returned to the castle after Lord Cedrik took his place, but Cedrik and I became close simply because we were the two loners. For some reason, Cedrik found it easy to talk to me. We had long discussions that continued late into the night. We went through Lord Cathal's library, reading the books about the history of the vampires. We had debates and discussions about the course of history and we agreed on most things, both of us taking the human view. Cedrik never really saw himself as a vampire, you see. He told me that the only time he had fed on human blood was when he was with you in your castle. He had learned a better way, he said, when the two of you were travelling to Zwischenmeer and you taught him to survive by drinking the blood of animals. He knew that you thought it was uncouth and an unworthy meal, only suitable for travelling when the human blood ran out, but he saw it as his salvation. If he never had to kill a human, he could deny his vampiric side. This system worked well for him for over a year. The villagers were provided with Geschenk credit for goods and services that they provided to the castle. In this way, they were able to barter between each other and pretend that they had no debt to the Vampire Lord of their village. This changed, however."

"One day, a small girl from the village arrived home with an animal bite. The girl's parents cleaned and bandaged the wound themselves, as the villagers had been all avoiding coming to Lord Cedrik for any healing since he had arrived. The girl soon began showing signs of illness, however. Her parents waited until she was very near death before bringing the girl to the castle. I am sure that Cedrik truly wanted to help the girl, but he took only a few steps toward her before he stopped. The girl's parents were begging him to help, to save their daughter, but Cedrik just stood there. I now believe it was because, after a year or more of subsisting on only animal blood, the temptation to drink from the young girl was too great. He was afraid that if he got too close to her, he would give in to temptation and drain her. In reality, the result would have been the same either way. The girl died in the arms of her parents."

"It was like the aftermath of the plague all over. The villagers blamed Cedrik for the girl's death. Despite the fact that they had avoided him, had not served him like they were supposed to since his arrival, they blamed him for not saving her. This time, however, there was no Blood Bank to destroy. They began attacking the castle, and Cedrik fended off most of the attacks using the Emotional Influence. Finally, however, after months of random acts of violence, after being deserted by every house servant except for me, three men finally succeeded in breaking into the castle one night. I didn't see what happened – I was in bed until I heard the screams. I rushed downstairs to find Cedrik leaning over the bodies of the men, draining the last of them. His thirst had finally beaten him."

Lord Radek had been silent up to this point, seemingly enthralled by the story. "But that was a good thing. Animal blood can help you to survive, but it is the human blood that makes you strong."

"Well," continued Hillard, "I don't know if Cedrik even knew that human blood would make him stronger. If he did, I doubt he would have cared. I think that, after that incident, Cedrik felt his last bit of humanity slipping away from him. He cried that night, raging against himself, calling himself a monster. He blamed you for everything. He wanted to kill you for making him into a monster. He wanted you to pay for, not only the deaths of his parents, but for making him into a killer as well. It was then that he was contacted by the Vampire Council." Hillard looked up, his eyes meeting those of Lord Radek, wondering what he would make of this new information.

Lord Radek was so still that he seemed almost to be made of stone. Hillard could see him thinking and wondered if Radek could even imagine what the Council had told Cedrik.

"The Vampire Council contacted Cedrik," the words came out of Radek like a sigh. "I never knew. In all of my communications with the Council since then, I have never had an inkling that they had communicated with Cedrik before he died."

"That's because they never wanted you to know," said Hillard.

Radek's eyes quickly shot up to meet those of Hillard. "What do you know of it?" he demanded.

Hillard paused for a few moments, enjoying the sight of Lord Radek squirming.

"You called me a rogue when I first arrived. That title would only have been correct if my creation had not been approved of by the Vampire Council."

"I know what I am," Hillard continued. "I have outlived many of the people I once knew. I have fed on humans only when needed, and then only sparingly. Those were the conditions placed on me by the Council when I was created."

"But, why do you not rule Zwischenmeer if the Council approved your creation?" Lord Radek seemed genuinely confused by now.

"They gave me another job. They did not trust you to place another vampire in Cedrik's place – I am sure you expected that after his death. They sent one of their own to rule the village. And they sent me here to be their spy."

Lord Radek sat back in his seat. Hillard just imagined the thoughts that were running through his head at this point. Lord Radek knew that he was breaking most of the Vampire Code in the way he was ruling Donner. In fact, he was paying the travelling merchants that passed through high prices to be quiet about the goings on in the village. Now he had just learned that it had all been for nought.

"Why should I believe you? You might just be trying to save your own skin. If you could make me believe that you were sent by the Council then I would never dare to kill you. The only problem is, if they knew what was going on in this village, they would never let things stay this way for so long. You would have been ordered to kill me long ago."

Hillard just smiled at Lord Radek. "You mean because of your harsh way of dealing with criminals? Your practice of taking the fog travellers as your own personal food supplement, instead of integrating them into the village to prop up the population? Those practices they could overlook. They know that these lands across the ocean are wild, and they can forgive harsh practices in a harsh land, as long as the human population does not drop too much. But, they could not forgive the creation of a true rogue."

Hillard had known that Christine was a vampire at the same time the Council had become aware. New vampires were never very good at protecting their thoughts, projecting them all over the place, if they had not been properly trained in how to shield them before being turned. Hillard had spent most of the walk from Adelaide's hide out to the castle, mentally pleading with the council to spare Christine's life. They still had not made a final decision. The lone female member of the Council was supporting Hillard's plea on the grounds that the number of female vampires was extremely low. They were withholding their final judgment until they could determine how Christine was adjusting to the change.

Lord Radek was just sitting in his seat, stunned that Hillard knew about Christine. He had greatly underestimated the power of the Council. All of his plans were coming down around his shoulders. He would not allow Hillard to kill Christine!

Lord Radek jumped up from his seat and faced Hillard. "I cannot allow you to harm her," he said. He opened a small drawer in the table in front of him and withdrew a wooden stake and quickly threw it at Hillard, aiming for the chest, expecting to surprise him and paralyze him with the wound.

Hillard was expecting something of the sort from Lord Radek, however, and jumped aside, pulling a stake of his own that had been tucked into the back waistband of his pants. As he did so, however, the thrust from Radek caught him on the shoulder and dug deep into the muscle. When Hillard pulled the wood from the wound, blood gushed out before the wound healed itself.

Hillard was grateful at this moment that you couldn't kill a vampire by simply injuring him once. It would take a significant number of such injuries to weaken him.

This small injury did not even slow him however, and Hillard quickly struck out at Radek. His opponent was quicker, however. The gift of age and a plentiful supply of human blood provided Radek with the upper hand over Hillard. Hillard repeatedly tried to get a strike through Radek's defences, but the older vampire was just too fast. Radek, however, hit Hillard again and again, until he was starting to feel the effects of blood loss.

He had come here to kill Radek, for the Council and for Adalaide, but he was not succeeding. If he wanted to have the chance to try again, he had to flee now. Knowing that the girls had had plenty of time to escape, he threw out the last shocking bit of information he had, trying to buy himself a break to escape.

"I was never going to harm Christine. She's gone now. Not even you can reach her!"

That stopped Radek in his tracks. Hillard took the two second reprieve to flee from the room and out of the castle. Radek must have gone straight to Christine's room, because Hillard heard him calling for her as he ran through the village and into the woods.

# Chapter 14

It took the girls a few hours to get Gervis back to Adelaide's hideout. They had considered taking him directly to his parents' house but, Sarah was surprised to learn, his parents were Gerwin and Elke and they lived too far out of town. Gervis needed time to recover from his blood loss before attempting that sort of extensive journey.

Christine looked over at Gervis occasionally with a haunted look on her face. Her thirst was an agony inside her, but seeing Gervis, someone she had almost killed, gave her the willpower to resist it. When they arrived at the hideout, she went to sit in a corner by herself, trying to block out the presence of the humans in the room.

Sarah looked over at Christine with concern. Unlike the other times in their lives when things had been hard, she just didn't know how to help her sister to deal with this. She wanted to go to

Christine, wrap her arms around her sister, and promise her that everything would be okay as long as they stayed together, but she was afraid that close contact might awaken Christine's thirst. She tried to focus on other things instead. The first thing she did was make Gervis comfortable in the lone bed in the room. Then she went over and sat down beside Adalaide.

There had been one train of thought circling her brain during the entire walk back to the hide away. Hillard was a vampire. He drank blood. He could affect her emotions. She didn't know what was real and what wasn't anymore. Oh, she knew that this world she was in was real. There was no more kidding herself that it was some kind of hallucination. She wasn't even sure when she had accepted the truth. The bigger problem now was that she didn't know who Hillard was anymore. Of course, they had only known each other for a few days. You never really know someone after such a short time. But even her first impressions were now called into doubt. Was he a nice guy – or did he make her feel safe around him by messing with her feelings? Were the warm feelings she had for him simply a fabrication?

Adalaide was sitting beside her, quietly looking from Sarah to Christine, who she was watching warily. Sarah finally looked her in the eyes and asked "You knew Hillard is a vampire?"

"Yes," Adalaide replied simply.

"How could you be friends with a monster?" Sarah decided that the straight-forward route was the best.

"How can you be sisters with a monster?" Adalaide retorted.

That set Sarah aback. She had to think about things, learn more about this. She looked over at Christine, who was now rocking back and forth in the corner, moaning.

"Christine, honey. It's going to be okay. I'm here for you. We can get through any…" She tried to put her arms around her sister but Christine pushed her away with supernatural strength and Sarah slammed back against the wall.

"Don't touch me!" she shrieked. "Don't you understand?! I'm *so* thirsty! And there is so much *blood* in this room." Suddenly, she stood up and began to stride towards the door. "I have to get out of here. You can't trust me Sarah. I have to go. Just look at Gervis. I couldn't stand it if I hurt you."

Just as she reached the door she stopped and took a step back. A second later the door opened and there stood Hillard. He and Christine just stared into each other's emerald eyes for a moment before he asked, "And where do you think you're going?"

"I have to get out of here. I might hurt them. You *know* that! Let me out."

Hillard looked over at the bed and saw Gervis. "Is he okay?"

Adalaide answered. "She nearly drained him right after she turned, but she stopped herself. Giselle made me take him with us. We have to warn his parents that Lord Radek will be coming for them."

Hillard nodded curtly. After a few seconds of thought, he took Christine's hand. "I know how to help you. Come with me. We'll go to warn Gerwin and Elke and we'll find you something to drink."

Christine looked panicked for a second. "I don't want to hurt anyone," she whimpered.

Hillard pulled her into a hug. "It's okay. You're going to be alright. You won't have to hurt anyone, I promise." As he hugged Christine, he looked over her shoulder at Sarah. Her face showed how betrayed she felt. Hillard didn't know what to say to her. He would just have to take care of her sister. He led Christine out of the shelter and they set off.

Adalaide had been watching the interplay between Sarah and Hillard. Now she waited to see what Sarah's reaction would be to seeing him again after discovering his true nature.

Sarah sat numbly for a minute. It was a shock to see him again. When their eyes had met, she had felt that same jolt of attraction she had been feeling all the time with him. Was it real? Or was it simply what he wanted her to feel? It wasn't important right now, she reminded herself. Christine was the most important thing to her now.

"Where are they going?" she asked Adalaide in a very subdued voice.

"Where he said. They are going to warn Gerwin and Elke." Adalaide was a little irritated with Sarah for even asking. Hillard would never lie.

"How can she drink and not hurt anyone? I thought they needed blood to survive."

"Humans are not the only animals with blood," Adalaide snapped at her. "Hillard does not drink human blood. Did you really think that he would? You have spent days with him and he has been nothing but protective of you. Do you really think that he would ever hurt anyone?"

Sarah was shocked at Adalaide's tone. Then she reminded herself that Adalaide and Hillard had a relationship. "I *don't* know him. That's the point. How do I know if anything he's shown me has been real? He can make me feel anything he wants. And you – how can you be with someone who is like that – a monster?!"

Now Adalaide was the one who was shocked. Then she chuckled. "Hillard and me?" She snorted. "Not in a million years. But," she interrupted before Sarah could speak "not because he is a 'monster' as you call him. Hillard is the most kind, gentle, honourable soul I have ever met – he is just not my type. I prefer the big, muscular, wood-cutter type of man. Hillard's a bit scrawny for my taste. Although," she said with a twinkle in her eye, "he *is* stronger than any wood-cutter I have ever met."

"How do you know that it's really him and not what he has made you think of him?"

"It does not work that way. They can affect your emotions when you are in their presence, but not when you are apart. I can understand you doubting him, things have been pretty strange for you in the past few days, but I care about him, and if you hurt him you will have to deal with me." Adalaide smirked. "And, while I am not a vampire, I am not always so gentle or honourable."

"Me? Hurt him?" Sarah had no idea what Adalaide meant. While she had a lot of extra weight, she was the first to admit that it was all fat. She was no physical threat to anyone.

"He cares about you, Sarah," Adalaide said gently, suddenly realizing that Sarah really had no idea of how Hillard really felt about her. "He has real, romantic feelings about you. Just because he is a vampire does not mean that he cannot care about someone and have his heart broken."

Sarah was dumbstruck. Sure, she and Hillard had had their moments. But he had always pulled away.  First she had thought it was because she wasn't pretty enough, or thin enough, then she had just assumed that it was because he and Adalaide had a relationship.

"How do you know that? He always pulls away as soon as we start to get close."

Adalaide smiled grimly at Sarah. "He has been afraid of how you would react when you found out what he was. And," she continued, a disapproving tone to her voice, "he thinks that because he is a vampire, he can *never* have a relationship."

"Well," said Sarah, stubbornly, "maybe he shouldn't.  What if the temptation got to be too great? What if he accidentally killed someone?"

Adalaide looked at Sarah with a fierce expression. "You had better not *ever* say anything like that to him.  That is his greatest fear.  But let me tell you, I have never met *anyone* with as much self-control as Hillard has."

The way she said that made Sarah pause. "What do you mean by that?"

Adalaide looked at the floor, and then looked up at Sarah. "I do not think he would want me to tell you this, but it will prove my point. I said that he drinks animal blood, but sometimes he needs something more. For some reason, if a vampire does not get at least small amounts of human blood, the blood thirst becomes irresistible. I have let him feed on me sometimes to regain his strength."

Sarah was shocked. "Why would you do that? You said you weren't in a relationship with him. What would make you want to do something like that?"

"I said he was my friend. He is. And he is going to help me get my revenge on Lord Radek. We have just been waiting for the day that Lord Radek steps over the line and the Vampire Council gives the word that he has to be destroyed. That word came this morning. I did not know for sure until I saw your sister, but I suspected when Hillard started sharpening sticks on the walk to the castle."

"So, Hillard is not a rogue?"

"No. And I do not know what happened at the castle, if he had the chance to go after Lord Radek. I do not think so though, not if he left here in such a hurry to warn Gerwin and Elke. That means that, at the very least, Lord Radek knows that Hillard is out to get him and is extremely angry. Most likely, he is out on the hunt for us all right now."

Sarah looked towards the door and shuddered. She hoped that she never had to see that monster again. Hillard and Christine may not be monsters, but the way that Lord Radek had looked at her, and what he had done to her sister, proved that Lord Radek definitely was.

"Adalaide, why do you want Radek dead so badly?"

Adalaide paused and took a deep breath. "He is responsible for the death of my parents."

Sarah just stared at Adalaide and, seeing the pain in her eyes, waited for her to continue.

"When I was fifteen, a merchant train came through Donner," she began. "There were some rougher than normal types with them.  Two of them started bothering my mother and I when we were in town buying some cloth for a new dress for me. My mother tried to stop them and they knocked her to the ground, tearing her dress. I ran into a nearby store to get help and came across my father. My father ran out into the street and caught the men trying to rape my mother. He fought them off of her and took her home. That night, Lord Radek came to our house and took my father away. As a punishment for fighting, he drained all of the men involved, including my father."

Sarah was shocked. Hillard had described such things to her, but when they had talked about it, it was just a hypothetical situation. She could not believe that such a thing had happened to Adalaide's family.

"And what happened to your mother?" Sarah was almost afraid to ask.

"Oh, Lord Radek had no excuse to punish her. Even he could not claim that being raped is a crime. He left my mother alone. But that did not console her. She felt responsible for my father's death and sunk into a deep depression. One day, she left our cabin and never came back. Some of the villagers found her at the bottom of a high cliff." Tears were now flowing down Adalaide's cheeks. "I have lived in their cabin ever since. I pay my one Geschenk a year for my land, but I grow the rest of my food and catch my meat. I will not give that monster one more drop of blood than I have to."

The two women just sat in silence. Sarah could completely understand Adalaide's need for revenge. She felt a very similar need herself, for what the monster had done to her sister.

Hillard and Christine made good time on the way to Elke and Gerwin's cottage. They stopped every so often so that Hillard could teach her how to find animals to drink from. The small animals she could drain, and bring back to the others as food, he explained. The large ones she could practice taking only a small drink from. It would never remove the thirst for human blood, but he explained that there were ways around that too.

Christine surreptitiously watched Hillard the whole time. Who was this vampire who had rescued her sister and was now teaching her to feed from animals, not humans? Was it possible that she could be a vampire and not hurt people?

Hillard was all too aware of her scrutiny. He had been giving periodic updates to the Vampire Council. They wanted to know if Christine would be a suitable replacement for Lord Radek. He still wasn't completely sure. She was listening very carefully to everything he was teaching her, but he wasn't sure how she was dealing with the situation as a whole. He wondered if she would be able to accept who and what she was now. He wanted to ask her about her sister, but was afraid to hear the answers. Things were confusing for him right now too. The moment that he and Sarah had shared before entering the castle had made him very aware that he had real feelings developing for the woman. Part of him wanted so much to share himself with her honestly and to be *with* someone for a change, instead of living on the outskirts of humanity. But the other part of him knew that it was a bad idea. He was basically immortal. She would live another twenty or thirty years. The temptation to turn her would be too great for him to resist. Of course, if he could prepare Christine enough so that she could take over the leadership of Donner, the Vampire Council would most likely send him somewhere else – somewhere far away from Sarah. The whole idea of being away from her made him hurt inside. He hadn't realized that it was possible for him to care for someone this way.

He shook his head. What he had to focus on now was Christine. He needed to help her to find a way to accept her new life so that she could be a suitable leader for Donner – and he had to do it fast. That was the least he could do for Sarah – make sure that her sister was not destroyed. Knowing that he would be the one ordered to destroy Christine made his mission all the more vital.

Finally, they reached Gerwin and Elke's cottage. The lights were on inside and everything seemed quiet. It appeared that they had made it to the cottage ahead of Lord Radek. Perhaps, in his dismay to discover that Christine and Sarah had escaped, the additional escape of Gervis had gone unnoticed. If that was the case, it was a good thing that they had arrived now. Lord Radek was sure to make the connection soon.

Hillard knocked on the door. Elke answered. She was in a long white nightgown and she looked shocked to see Hillard at the door. She was even more shocked to see Christine – and she nearly fell over when she saw Christine's emerald gaze looking back at her.

"Hillard! What has happened!? Is Gervis okay?" Suddenly, Gerwin was beside his wife in the doorway, looking concerned.

"He's alright now, Elke. But he's no longer at the castle. We have him somewhere safe, but Lord Radek is bound to be coming after the two of you next. The Vampire Council has decided that he is to be eliminated, so the threat to you and yours should be over soon, but you need to get somewhere safe in the meantime. Do you have a place to go?"

The elderly couple looked at each other and nodded. "We do," replied Gerwin gruffly. "You're sure Gervis is okay?" He looked suspiciously at Christine, who looked away from him, shame painting her face.

"He'll be fine. He just needs a bit of rest. As I said, this should all finally be over for you soon. I know the last fifteen years have been hell for you, but you've done what you had to do to survive." Hillard looked pointedly at Gerwin, who seemed to take what Hillard said to heart.

Gerwin looked more kindly upon Christine and asked, "And how is your sister? Is she okay?"

"She's better than I am," she said, in her own way trying to tell the couple that her sister had not been turned like she had.

Gerwin and Elke both nodded. Hillard took Christine's arm and led her down the stairs. "They'll need to get out of here. Let's go and let them do what they need to."

Hillard had shown her several things besides hunting on their journey to Gerwin and Elke's cottage. First was the fact that she could now run extremely fast, and without seeming to get tired. Hillard told her that she *would* get tired, eventually, but that her stamina was dependant on the amount of blood she had consumed recently. Another thing he had demonstrated was her new strength. She could lift enormous objects now. It was like she had suddenly become a bodybuilder overnight. That part of it was a bit of a thrill.

She was wondering now why they were walking at such a normal pace, until Hillard moved off the main road and led her into a clearing.

"This is where your sister and I spent some time the day after I found her," he said. "I thought we could sit here for a while and talk about whatever is on your mind. I've seen you stealing glances at me all night. I'm sure you have a lot of questions. I think it's better if we do a lot of this talking before we get back to the others. They're probably all sleeping by now anyway, so we have time."

Christine indeed had many questions swirling around in her brain. She asked the first one that came to mind. "What did you mean when you told Gerwin and Elke that they had only done what they'd had to do to survive? Did that have something to do with Sarah and I?"

Hillard nodded slowly. This was a question he had been expecting. "Lord Radek took Gervis from them when he was just a boy. When he was young, they lived with him in the village, but when he turned ten, Lord Radek took him from them and told them that they had to move out here. Their job was to find the fog travellers, keep them calm, and send them on towards Donner where he or his soldiers would find them and bring them to the castle dungeons."

"But that's horrible! How could they do that, knowing that the people they sent on would be killed by Lord Radek?"

"They really had no choice, Christine. He had their son. They couldn't flee to another settlement without Gervis, and if they refused, Lord Radek would kill all three of them. They were trapped. Living so far out of town, they had only each other. It would take them more than a day to get into town, and at the age they are now, they can't make that trip anymore. The only communication they have is with me, Adalaide, and when Lord Radek comes once a month, just before the fog, to remind them of their responsibilities, to bring them some extra supplies, and to exchange letters with them for Gervis."

"He acts as a postman for them?" Christine could not imagine Lord Radek doing something so kind and thoughtful.

"Don't mistake it for what it isn't. He brings them a letter from their son to remind them of their responsibility to him and to their son. It's a reminder of what they have to lose should they try to betray him."

Christine thought for a bit about the couple and her and Sarah's strange initial visit with them. It so seemed obvious to her now that they had been hiding something. It was also obvious that they had tried, in the most subtle of ways, to warn them. She couldn't blame them for trying to protect their son — especially since she had so recently come close to killing him herself. She was far from blameless herself in this situation.

Christine sighed, half in despair. "How do they get away with all of this? The Vampire Lords, I mean. And why are you and I able to see that it is so wrong when we are … like them?" She couldn't yet face calling herself a vampire.

Hillard smiled at her and shook his head. "Not all vampires are like Lord Radek, Christine. In fact, very few villages are as bad as this one. Lord Radek is very old. He was from the first batch of vampires, a group that went crazy in their blood lust, drinking more than their fill every day until the human population was decimated. He has always resented the fact that there are rules now and that he has limits. He feels that he is better than all of the lowly humans, because he's stronger than they are, and faster, and can make them feel however he wants them to. What he doesn't realize is that he needs them. If there were no humans, he would quickly die. We can live on animal blood but, Christine, we need a certain amount of human blood to keep ourselves sane. I don't know why that is." He smiled. "They say you are what you eat."

Christine gasped at the horrible joke and then smiled back at him warily. "But how can you drink human blood? I thought you didn't hurt anyone."

"You met Adalaide?"

Christine nodded.

"She and I have a bit of a symbiotic relationship. I bring her the wild animals that I kill and about once a month or so, she gives me a very small drink. It is not a lot. It is just enough to keep the thirst at bay, so that I don't crave the human blood so much, so that I can walk among people without worrying that I'll hurt them."

Christine looked at him. "And she lets you do this?" She was remembering the times that Lord Radek had drunk from her. At the moment it was occurring it was pleasant, but that was because he affected her emotions at the time. Afterwards she had felt violated.

Hillard seemed to read her thoughts. "If it is done willingly, as a gift, it's okay. That is where the word Geschenk comes from. It means gift. And I don't drink from her directly. She makes a small cut on her wrist and lets the blood run into a glass. When the glass is about one quarter full, I put a drop of my blood on her cut and it heals. That is the way it is supposed to be done."

Christine nodded. It almost made sense that way. And it was similar the scene depicted on the tapestry in her room in the castle.

"What are the other villages like?" she asked.

Hillard was glad that she had asked this question. It gave him the opportunity to approach the subject of leadership without mentioning it first. The Vampire Council could not chastise him for answering a question and it made Christine look like a better candidate for leadership in their eyes for asking the question in the first place.

"Well, they are each a little different. Each leader approaches things in their own way. The best, happiest villages are run by leaders who understand the value of humanity. They understand that the sacrifices the humans make to give the Geschenk require them to give back to the community as well. Some villages love their leaders. Some merely tolerate them. Some, like Donner, hate them. I know that the vampire stories in your world depict us as monsters, Christine, but it doesn't have to be that way. We have a lot to offer humanity. We have the power to heal."

Christine was nodding. "Lord Radek told me that." Thinking about him, Christine felt a little guilty for abandoning him. "Hillard, he came to me in my room last night. He told me that he was lonely. He said that if Sarah and I stayed with him as his companions, he would never feed on us. I still don't know if he was telling the truth."

Hillard had been able to sense that something was bothering Christine. He tried to console her. "It's most likely that he was planning to turn you from the start, Christine. The Vampire Council has suspected for a long time that his increased blood lust was leading up to him making a play for power. I believe, as they do, that he would have turned you and then forced you to feed on both Sarah and Gervis, to remove your final attachments to humanity and tie you that much closer to him."

Christine had to admit that it was possible. Lord Radek's sudden interest in gaining her friendship had not seemed completely genuine to her. She knew that it was likely that she would never learn the truth now. Not only had she tried to escape before he turned her, but she had then successfully ran away with Sarah afterwards as well. And now the Vampire Council wanted him dead for turning her without permission.

She gasped at the thought and asked, "Does the Vampire Council want me destroyed because Radek made *me* without permission?" It was a surprising thought, but one she should have had before this.

Hillard had been dreading this question. The Vampire Council still had not made a decision, although throughout this conversation with Christine he had been in almost constant communication with them. The general opinion at this point was that she seemed to be adjusting well, but that it was still too soon to make a final determination. They reminded him that he was not to tell her that she was being considered for a leadership position, or even that they were trying to decide whether or not to let her live.

"I don't know. I hope they'll let you live. Sarah would never forgive me if anything happened to you." His shoulders slumped. "She might not forgive me for not telling her what I was. For all I know, she hates me now."

Christine stared at him. Was he telling her what she thought he was telling her?

"You have feelings for my sister?" she asked quietly.

Hillard took a deep breath. "Yes. I know I have no right to, but she's so strong and opinionated," he smiled, "she has nearly bitten my head off a few times for saying stupid things." He thought again for a moment. "Sometimes, though, she seems so vulnerable."

Christine nodded. She knew all too well about Sarah's vulnerability. The strong pig-headed part of her was more of a defence mechanism than anything else.

"She had a pretty hard time of it when we were kids," she started to explain. "Our dad was a bit of a drunk. Okay, he was a lot of a drunk, and Sarah was his favourite target when things weren't going his way. He was always proud of the fact that he never hit us, but I think that his words cut Sarah deeper than any physical violence ever could. He called her fat and ugly on a regular basis. He compared her to farm animals and basically cut any self confidence that she had to shreds. By the time he died, she had become a self-fulfilling prophecy, eating to comfort herself from the pain of living with him. She has never been able to let go of the vision of herself that he planted in her brain. No matter how much weight she has lost, or how terrific she looks, what she sees in the mirror is an ugly fat girl, not worth anyone's attention or love. The fact that she just caught her husband cheating on her has only compounded the situation."

Hillard understood everything now. He now recognized the scared look in her eyes every time he tried to tell her how lovely he found her. The walls that she had built up around herself had only grown stronger since her husband had betrayed her. Hillard felt ashamed that he may have compounded the problem by sending mixed messages to her. Of course, it didn't make his situation any easier. Either he could try to have a relationship with her — one doomed to failure because he was a monster in her eyes — or he could push her away — and make her feel even more rejected and worthless. He only hoped that the Vampire Council spared Christine. He could not bear to see the look in her eyes if he were forced to kill her sister.

He stood up. "Time to get back. We should check on everyone else and maybe check on the village to see what Radek is up to."

Christine nodded. She wanted to check on Gervis. Now that she'd had time to think she knew that she had to try to make things up to him. She couldn't just leave things as they were. It was so sad that things would never develop further between the two of them – that possibility had died when she had almost killed him. Now she just had to try to make amends, if there was any way to make amends for drinking almost all of someone's blood.

The two vampires headed off into the dark of the night, using all of the superhuman speed available to them.

# Chapter 15

Sarah sat in the dimly lit room and kept watch as Adelaide and Gervis slept. Gervis had awoken only briefly, eating a small amount of food and drinking some water, before falling back asleep. He still seemed to be quite weak, but was slowly improving. What had surprised Sarah most, however, was that he had seemed very concerned about Christine. He didn't even seem to consider her at fault for nearly killing him. He seemed only to be concerned with her wellbeing. Perhaps it had something to do with the fact that he had spent the last fifteen years living with a vampire. Maybe he *expected* to have his blood taken like that. Sarah shook her head. She still didn't understand the complexities of living in this world.

Suddenly, she heard footsteps outside. She shook Adalaide awake and they both kept their eyes glued to the door, Sarah holding her knife and Adalaide holding a sword at the ready. They both fervently hoped that it was nothing more than Hillard and Christine returning from their trip to warn Gervis' parents.

The door opened. The face that peaked in was one unknown to Sarah, but Adalaide smiled widely. "Conrad!  What are you doing here?"

Giselle followed Conrad into the small room. They looked grim.

"It is a terrible thing," began Conrad. "After you left, Lord Radek flew into a terrible rage. He killed all of his guard staff." He turned a stern look to Giselle. "I have told my wife more than a dozen times not to mess with the Lord when he is angry."

Giselle turned an indignant look to her husband. "Well, I never thought he would do me any harm!" Her look softened in chagrin. "At least not until now."

Adalaide looked in shock at the pair. "Tell me what happened."

"Well," explained Giselle, "I went down to the guard house this morning to see why none of the boys had come to breakfast." Her face turned white at the memory. "They were all dead. Every one of them. Pale and cold in their beds, their throats torn and empty of blood. It was a horror! I ran straight out of the castle to Conrad."

Sarah and Adalaide just stared at Giselle in horror. They could not believe that Lord Radek had begun killing his own men.

Conrad spoke. "It just gets worse. Just after Giselle told me what she had found, I looked out the window and saw Lord Radek, going door to door, leading the villagers towards the castle. I tell you, I knew he was up to no good, so I grabbed Giselle and we ran out of the village and straight here."

"The villagers? Has anyone gone to warn my parents?" a weak voice asked from the bed.

"Oh, you dear boy!" Giselle ran to Gervis' side. "Well, you're looking much better! You had me worried you know. I don't know what I would have done if she had … " Giselle left the final words unspoken, but the 'killed you' echoed off the walls of Sarah's mind.

Sarah rested a reassuring hand upon Gervis' head. "Hillard and Christine went. I'm sure they got there in time."

Gervis' eyes lit up at Christine's name and he tried to get up. "Are they back yet? I want to talk to her – I have to tell her that I don't blame her."

Giselle looked like she was about to speak. Sarah cut her off before she could say anything negative about Christine. "She isn't back yet, but I promise I'll tell her.  You just get some rest, okay? If you want her to feel better, show her how much better you're feeling."

Gervis nodded weakly and fell back against the pillow. In only a few seconds, he was asleep again.

Giselle looked angrily at Sarah.  "I know she is your sister, but she almost killed that boy! There is no way she should be getting anywhere near him again!"

"I understand how you feel, Giselle.  It's obvious to me that he's like a son to you.  But you have to let him make the choice.  I'm having a hard enough time accepting what happened to my sister. I want to wait and see what happens. From what Adalaide told me, there is no reason that Christine should suddenly become evil. Hillard is a wonderful person." As the words left her mouth, Sarah realized that she believed them. She liked Hillard as a person, even when he wasn't in the room.  She smiled at Giselle, who remained angry.

"I know that Hillard is nice enough. But how do we know that he is not the exception. The only other vampire I have seen before him was Lord Radek, and look what he's doing now!"

Sarah wished that Christine and Hillard would return quickly. As if in answer to her prayers, footsteps sounded outside and the door opened again. Hillard and Christine came into the overcrowded room. Christine looked much calmer than she had when they had left several hours earlier.  Sarah decided to take that as a good sign.

Hillard walked over to Conrad and shook his hand. They nodded at each other in greeting.

"Let me introduce everyone," Adalaide offered, "I think everyone knows Hillard." Everyone smiled. "This is Conrad, Giselle's husband and the village blacksmith. He has made all of the fine weaponry you find on the wall behind me. Conrad was a good friend of my father and he and Giselle have been watching out for me since my parents died." She smiled warmly at Conrad. "Conrad tried to talk me out of taking on Lord Radek when I first told him my plan, but when he discovered that he could not talk me out of it, he decided to properly outfit me instead." The two hugged warmly.

"Conrad," she continued, "this is Sarah and her sister Christine. I am sure you have heard an earful about Christine from Giselle," she winked at Giselle's sour expression upon hearing Christine's name, "but I have heard a lot about her from her sister, and a little from Gervis too, so I do not think she is all bad." Adalaide smiled warmly at Christine to show her that she was welcome.

Giselle sniffed and looked over at Christine. "We'll see how you turn out," she said suspiciously. Everyone chuckled a bit, and even Christine smiled faintly at the brusque words.

"I understand how you feel, Giselle. I'm the reason that Gervis is lying there." A pleading look entered Christine's now emerald eyes, "but I promise that I will spend the rest of my life trying to make it up to him." Giselle nodded tersely, satisfied for the moment.

Adalaide moved on to business. "Hillard, Lord Radek is rounding up the villagers. I think he means to kill them all."

Hillard nodded. He had been afraid of something like this. If Radek drained all of the villagers, his strength would increase ten-fold. It would take the entire Vampire Council to take him down. There had to be a way to stop him. He sent a silent mental inquiry to the Council, hoping that they would have an idea, but all they could suggest was having he and Christine go after Radek together, after making sure that they were at their full power.

He closed his eyes for a moment. He didn't know how to broach this subject.

"The Vampire Council has said that Christine and I need to go after Radek alone. We are the only ones who even come close to his strength."

"I am coming with you," insisted Adelaide. "This is my fight too."

Hillard smiled at her. "I doubt I could stop you."

"I'm coming too," said Sarah. Everyone turned to her.

Christine took her aside. "You can't help me this time, Sarah. I'd spend all of my time watching out for you. It would put us both in much more danger."

Sarah stepped back and looked at her little sister, as if only now seeing her for the first time. Usually it was Sarah who did the protecting, but now Christine had a new maturity in her eyes. "Okay," she admitted, "but I want to help."

"How?" asked Christine.

"I want you to take my blood. You need to have more strength to fight Lord Radek."

Christine looked horrified, but Hillard nodded. "It's what the Vampire Council said we should do, but I didn't know how to ask."

Conrad and Giselle quickly offered to have them drink a Geschenk from each of them as well, but Christine flatly refused. "I can't do it. I can't risk that I might lose control and drain you."

Hillard tried to explain that, because Christine had nearly drained Gervis earlier (she turned ashen and winced when she was reminded of that) and had drunk from so many forest animals, there was no chance of the thirst taking over. She would have full control. Even so, she refused to go near her sister, finally agreeing after much arguing to take a small amount from Conrad. It was an astonishing sight for Sarah to watch, Christine taking Conrad's wrist in her hands and lowering her mouth to it. Sarah didn't see any wound and Conrad didn't even wince as Christine drank. It seemed like a painless procedure. She looked over at Hillard, who had just finished drinking from Giselle.

"If Christine won't drink from me, I want you to," Sarah insisted, feeling that it was the right thing to do and wanting to be of some help to the trio.

Hillard stared deeply into her eyes for a moment. There were so many emotions whirling around in his emerald orbs that, for a moment, Sarah felt herself get lost in his gaze.

Finally, Hillard nodded. Sarah held her wrist out to him and he took it gently in his hands. He lifted it to his mouth and first kissed the inside of her wrist and palm gently, looking into her eyes. It was the only way he knew to tell her how grateful he was for this gift, how much he cared about her, and how much he wished that things could be different between them. Then he lowered his mouth to the vein and drank.

Sarah had expected to feel a twinge of pain as he opened her vein, but she felt nothing. She closed her eyes and concentrated on the feeling of his lips on her skin. It was something she had been subconsciously thinking about for days, but she had never expected it to happen like this. With her eyes closed, she concentrated on her inner emotions, wondering if he was using his influence to change the way she was feeling. She was shocked to find instead that she could feel what he was feeling. There was tenderness towards her, a deep gratitude, and … he had so many deep feelings for her, wonderful feelings, real feelings. For a moment she let herself go and allowed herself to feel truly loved for the first time in her life. She felt warm and safe and truly happy, and she knew that those were her own emotions, not those planted within her.

When she finally opened her eyes, Hillard, Christine and Adalaide were gone.

# CHAPTER 16

Hillard and Christine were walking at a brisk, but more normal pace, in order to allow Adalaide to keep up. They were silent, each lost in their own thoughts, until Hillard spoke.

"Since Lord Radek has killed his own guards, we can try scaling the walls. I would guess that Lord Radek will be distracted by whatever he is doing with the villagers." Hillard closed his eyes for a moment, trying not to picture the horrors that Lord Radek could be unleashing on the prisoners even now. "On the other hand, he is likely to be expecting us. He knows that the Vampire Council wants him dead and he knows that I'm the one coming after him. So, I think that it's best if only you two scale the walls. Adalaide, you take the northern wall and Christine, you take the southern wall. Adalaide will try to get to wherever the prisoners are being held and release them. Tell them to flee into the forest and to split up. If Lord Radek escapes us, then it will be harder for him to gather them all back up. The Vampire Council will come for him if we fail so he will be trying to obtain all of the human blood that he can to increase his strength."

"Christine, I want you to stay in the background." He held his hand up as she looked like she was about to protest. "I am going to tell him that I was ordered to kill you by the Vampire Council. That way, he won't expect you to be there to help me. I only want you to come to my aid if you think you can be of real help. If it looks hopeless, run back to the hideout and warn your sister and the others. They should have enough supplies to stay safe for the week or so until the Vampire Council arrives to take care of Lord Radek." Christine looked over at Adalaide, expecting a similar order for her. Adalaide smiled at her grimly.

"I have my own score to settle with Lord Radek. I am not leaving here unless he is dead." Christine's eyes widened as she realized the solemn implications of that statement.

The three split up – Hillard heading towards the front gate of the castle, and the girls flanking the castle on each side. Hillard hoped that his show of bravado at coming to the front gate would enrage Lord Radek and distract him from the girls coming up the walls. He knew that there was very little chance of success today. Lord Radek had been far more powerful than him in their battle yesterday, but he hoped against hope that he would be able to weaken him enough so that Christine or Adalaide could finish him. In the back of his mind, he worried that Christine would not be able to hurt anyone, not even the evil monster who had stolen her humanity, but he hoped that he was wrong.

Sarah was driving herself crazy, imagining what was going on at the castle without her. She feared not only for her sister, but for Hillard. In the brief moment of intimacy that they had shared before he left, he had shown her that he really did care for her.

Despite the overwhelming sense of weakness that enveloped her body, she knew that she had to go to the castle, if not to help, then at least to bear witness to the fate of the people she loved. She rushed from the hideaway, ignoring the protests of Giselle, Conrad and Gervis, and moved as quickly through the forest as her exhausted body would allow.

Hillard braced his shoulders and raised his head high, as he shouted his challenge towards the castle in front of him, "Radek! Are you really so afraid of me that you need to kill innocent villagers to strengthen yourself?!"

The castle was quiet for a moment, and then the face of Lord Radek looked over the wall directly above the front gate. "You know I have no fear of you, Hillard. You are weak and pathetic from drinking the blood of stupid animals. I am preparing to take over the Vampire Council. When they arrive I want to be ready to take my rightful place."

Hillard had suspected as much, so he wasn't surprised. He knew also, that Lord Radek could drink the blood of every villager in Donner and in several other villages and still not be close to the combined power of the Vampire Council. Lord Radek had somehow lost his grip on reality and the Vampire Council had made the right decision when they decided to have Lord Radek removed from power.

The heavy oak doors leading to the castle courtyard swung inwards and Hillard didn't hesitate before striding through. He looked to the left side of the courtyard and saw sixty or seventy villagers huddled in the corner. That was a good sign – the entire village, including the surrounding area, had almost six hundred inhabitants. There was no way that Radek could have killed that many and disposed of the bodies in such a short time, so it appeared that many of the villagers had already fled to safety.

The villagers who were there, however, looked at Hillard with a mix of hope and despair. He hoped that he would be able to save them.

Lord Radek took a giant leap down from the castle wall and stood in front of Hillard, a cocky expression on his face. "Why did you even come here? You know that you cannot beat me."

"I was ordered to try by the Vampire Council," Hillard replied, "I always do as I am ordered." He hoped that Lord Radek would catch the insinuation in his mocking tone.

Lord Radek took the bait. "What have you done with Christine!?" he demanded.

Hillard pretended to look sad and ashamed. "I didn't want to kill her. I have feelings for her sister. But I had to do as I was ordered. I took her into the woods last night and set her aflame."

Lord Radek's eyes widened in horror. "You destroyed her?! How could you do that? Were you blind to her perfect beauty? She was to be my queen!"

Hillard tried to grind some salt into the wound. "She begged for my mercy. She even tried to convince me not to kill you. She said that you were just lonely. But I knew the truth – you are mad, and you would have only infected her with your sickness!"

Lord Radek's emerald eyes flared in anger. He flew towards his opponent with such a speed that even Hillard had never encountered anything like it before. He struck Hillard full on, sending him flying into a tree on the other side of the courtyard.

Hillard's spinning head cleared after only a few moments. He reached up, and tore a branch from the tree. "You may be stronger, Radek, but I'm smarter – and not half as crazy." He had to add the last bit. Radek's anger was his weakness, Hillard had realized. The fight was on.

Adalaide saw no way for her to free the villagers without going down into the courtyard. She entered the guard's quarters and began making her way downstairs. She would come out into the courtyard behind the group of villagers and, if she were lucky, behind Radek. She stopped near the fireplace and picked up a longish piece of wood. She lit an oil lamp and carried that with her as well. She now had everything that she needed to finish off that bastard once and for all!

She slipped through the outer door to the guard house, careful to avoid being seen by Lord Radek. It wasn't difficult to avoid detection, as he appeared to be consumed with his battle with Hillard. The villagers looked surprised to see her, as she slipped between them, but were careful not to give her away. The tools that she carried were proof enough that she was here to save them.

Adalaide handed the oil lamp to Toby, the Baker's apprentice, with the whispered instructions to be ready to hand it to her as soon as she needed it.

The fight between Hillard and Lord Radek was moving towards the front doors to the castle, and Adalaide moved towards the front gate, in order to get a clear view of Radek when she was ready.

Sarah arrived at the castle and knew that the battle was still going on, by the crashing sounds she could hear coming from the courtyard. She didn't want to distract anyone and she knew that she would be of no help in the fight. Her breath was coming in short gasps from rushing and her head was spinning. She hid around the corner of the front gate and watched in horror as she saw the beating that Lord Radek was giving Hillard. She saw Adalaide come into view a few metres ahead of her and hoped that she had some idea of how to save Hillard and the others.

Christine watched the fight from the northern wall. She was touched by Lord Radek's dismay at her apparent demise, but was able to clearly see the madness that lurked within him.

Hillard appeared to be losing the battle. He could get nowhere near Lord Radek with the stake he had torn from the tree. Lord Radek's speed was incredible. He zoomed back and forth around Hillard, taunting him and knocking him repeatedly off of his feet.

Finally, after an incredibly hard hit that had Hillard bouncing off of the wall of the castle, knocking many of the bricks out of place, Lord Radek tore the stick from Hillard's grasp and stood above him, a triumphant smile on his face.

"You were no match for me," he gloated, "I do not even know why you tried."

Lord Radek thrust the stake through Hillard's heart and Hillard gasped and froze. He was unable to move, unable to communicate. With the stick preventing his heart from pumping his blood through his body, his power of regeneration was stilled.

Lord Radek looked down at him and sneered. "Now you are even more pathetic. I think I will go and find Christine's sister and drain her dry right in front of you. I will keep you alive just to torment you.   Then, I will burn you, like you burned my Christine."

"I do not think so," a strong female voice from behind him asserted.

Lord Radek spun around to find Adalaide standing there, a stake flying from her hand even as he turned, heading directly for his heart.  Instead of running, he grabbed a knife from a sheath on his hip and flung it at Adelaide. The blade pierced her lung and went clear through her body; the force of the throw magnified one hundred fold by the blood consumed by the Vampire Lord in the last twenty-four hours.

Despite the accuracy of his throw, Lord Radek had misjudged Adalaide's aim. The stake dug deep into his chest, not exactly piercing the centre of his heart, but hitting enough of it that he hit the ground like a tonne of bricks. He lay there, stunned and unable to move.

Christine leapt down from the castle wall and stood over Lord Radek. His eyes widened as he saw her.

"My love, you still live." Because the stake had not fully pierced his heart, Lord Radek was still capable of speech.

"If you can call this living." Christine spat at her maker. "You held me captive, drank my blood, and then you turned me into a monster like you. How can you call me your love? I wouldn't even inflict such a thing on someone I hated."

Lord Radek looked pleadingly at Christine. "All I wanted was a companion. You were to be my queen. We could still rule all of the Vampires together."

Christine looked coldly down at Lord Radek. "You threatened to kill my sister." She took a few steps back from him and flung a burning oil lamp down onto his prone, vulnerable body. Lord Radek's body caught aflame like a piece of dry parchment held over a candle. Within seconds, there was nothing left of him but ash.

"CHRISTINE." A voice sounded like thunder in her head. Her eyes widened in shock. "WE HAVE DECIDED THAT YOU MAY LIVE. YOUR ACTIONS REGARDING RADEK WERE

HONOURABLE AND RIGHT. DONNER WILL NEED A STRONG LEADER AND WE WOULD LIKE TO ASK YOU TO FULFILL THIS ROLE."

Christine was shaken. She had hoped that she would be allowed to live, but she had never expected this. "But I don't know how to lead," she protested, speaking aloud as telepathic communication was something Hillard had not taught her.

"HILLARD WILL GUIDE YOU IN THE BEGINNING."

"But Hillard is…"

"GO TO HIM, PULL OUT THE STAKE." With that final command, the connection was broken.

Christine did as she was told and Hillard blinked, took a deep breath, and rose. He ran over to Adalaide, hoping to save her life with his blood, but she was already dead. Tears in his eyes, he looked beyond her and saw a figure slumped in the doorway of the castle gate.

Hillard rushed over to see who it was, and his breath caught in his throat. It was Sarah. Tears were in her eyes and Lord Radek's knife was protruding from the side of her neck. She had been fighting the urge to pull it out, knowing that she would be dead within seconds if she did, but her blood was still in a huge pool around her.

"Oh Sarah," Hillard whispered. He wanted to take her in his arms, but that might just make things worse. There were very few injuries or diseases that a few drops of vampire blood could not cure. Someone who had very nearly bled to death was one. Vampire blood could not gather the blood from the stone around Sarah and put it back into her body. She had lost too much already to survive her injuries, even if they were healed. And vampire blood could not cure death.

"I'm cold," Sarah managed to whisper. Her eyes were so very tired.

Hillard didn't want to let her go – he had just found her. How could she die without learning how to love herself, without learning how much he loved her?

Suddenly Christine was beside him. "Can't you help her?" she pleaded.

"No. The blood. I can't put it back."

"Then give her yours." Christine's voice was flat and insistent.

Hillard looked at her. "You don't know what you're asking of me. She will be a rogue, like you were. There is nothing that will make the Vampire Council allow her to live. She will be as good as dead anyway."

"Then we hide her," Christine insisted.

"They'll be able to feel her." Hillard paused, and then looked down at Sarah, seeming caught between two decisions. "Can you hear me, Sarah?"

She gazed up into his eyes. "I'm dying, aren't I?" Her voice was barely audible.

Hillard took a deep breath. "You don't . . . have to. I can make you ... like me. I know you think I'm a monster, but *you* can be anything you want to be."

She looked at him, love in her eyes. "You're not . . . a monster. I know you would never hurt me. And I . . . don't want to die. Is it true that you don't have to . . . hurt people?" Her voice was getting weaker and Hillard was starting to fear that it would soon be too late to do anything.

"It's true. Sarah, if we do this, we need to hide you from the Vampire Council. Christine, listen to what I say, you'll have to shield your thoughts too. I need you both to visualize a solid brick wall around your mind. You need to make sure that you don't broadcast your thoughts to the Council unintentionally. Later I'll have more time to teach you. Do you think you can do that?"

Sarah just smiled at him weakly. Hillard didn't know if she had even heard him, but he couldn't let her go. He didn't want to be alone again. He took a deep breath and closed his eyes. Then he opened a wound in his left wrist and placed it to Sarah's mouth.

For a moment, he thought he was too late. Sarah's eyes were now closed and she didn't start drinking. Then, as a few drops of his blood slipped between her lips and down her throat, a minute amount of strength seemed to pull her back from the very brink of death. Her lips pressed lightly against his wrist at first, and then more urgently. After a moment, she finally stopped drinking and opened her eyes – her glowing emerald eyes.

If you loved

## THUNDER AND BLOOD

read on for a sneak peek at

# THUNDER AND ICE

The next chapter in the exciting
Thunder and Blood series

## by Stacey Voss

*Coming Spring 2010*

*Visit  www.thunderandblood.com for more
information.*

# THUNDER AND ICE
### *Coming Spring 2010*

Sarah stood at the window of the gorgeous bedroom and gazed out at the slowly rising sun as it ascended from behind the Sleeping Giant. It was hard to believe that only a week or so ago she had been watching practically the same scene from the comfort of her sister's apartment. The lives of her and her sister had changed so drastically since then that she'd had hardly enough time to catch her breath. When she had awoken yesterday morning, she had been human – now she was something more.

All she remembered of the time before her transformation was watching Hillard battle with Lord Radek, the insane ruler of the small village of Donner. Things had been going badly for Hillard and she had been about to try to help him (however futile that attempt might have been) when she had felt a sudden painful burning sensation in her neck. After that, she remembered nothing until she opened her eyes to see Hillard looking down at her in undisguised relief. It was then that she had first felt the craving. It had begun as a dryness that started deep within her soul, rapidly creeping outward to fill her entire being. It had felt as if she hadn't had a drop of water in days and had spent the last few weeks clawing her way through a vast dry desert. It was at that point that she remembered Hillard lifting her into his arms and racing with his unnatural speed into the forest.

Sarah was startled out of her reverie by a knock at the door, followed afew seconds later by her sister, Christine, entering the room. Christine was stunning in a green satin gown whose colour appeared almost drab when compared to her phenomenal emerald eyes. Her blond curls haloed her face and she looked like an angel.

"Hey. Whatcha doing? Are you tired?" she asked, appraising Sarah with a measured glance.

"Surprisingly not," Sarah replied, "or maybe not so surprising. I'm not sure *what* to expect now. I wish Hillard was around so I could ask him exactly what I should be doing now."

Christine looked distracted for a moment. "I think he just needed some time alone," she finally replied. "We've all had a rough time of it the last couple of days, especially Hillard. And remember, Hillard is used to being alone."

Christine was right. Hillard had been alone when Sarah had first met him. He had come to her rescue when she had been sick and alone and terribly worried about Christine, who had disappeared. He had stayed by her side almost constantly since then, first helping her to rescue her sister, then coming to the aid of the entire village by ridding them of the insane Lord Radek. After taking Sarah out to the woods to help her quench that overwhelming initial thirst, however, he had returned to the forest alone without a word. Sarah was surprised to feel a vast sense of emptiness inside her at his disappearance. She wondered if it was due to her new physical state or because of his simple absence from their newly blossoming relationship. They had shared a few special moments over the last few days and Sarah knew that he did have some strong feelings for her. She knew that he had been keeping her at arm's length because he felt that he shouldn't become involved with a human, but she was a vampire now too. Sarah hoped that he just needed some time to absorb everything that had happened over the last few days. Besides having changed her into a vampire in a moment of desperation to save her life, Hillard had also lost his closest friend, Adelaide, during the battle with Lord Radek.

Finally, Sarah sighed and said, "So, what's up? I take it you're not tired either. You wanna go out and test these new vampiric powers of ours?" She finally grinned at the entertaining idea of testing out the limits of her new body.

"I don't think that's a good idea. The sun's up, and while I know it won't kill us, I think we should wait until Hillard's home and we have a chance to talk to him before we start testing out the validity of all those old vampire myths."

"Home, hunh? I guess you're really settling into this whole Lady of the Manor thing." Sarah was still a little awed by the fact that her sister was now the local ruler.  It was just a small village, but it still wasn't what she ever would have expected from her baby sister.

The Vampire Council, sending their wishes to Hillard telepathically, had decided that Christine would be allowed to live, despite her having been turned into a vampire without their consent by the insane Lord Radek. In a further shocking development, they had decreed that Christine would rule in Radek's place, having proven herself capable of both rational thought and compassion toward others. In essence, the large ornate castle in which they now found themselves belonged to her, and the villagers that lived below and at the bottom of the hill, owed their fealty to her baby sister.

Christine snorted at Sarah's reference to her new status. "Hey, it's half yours too. Ruling a village is a lot different than running a classroom," she said in reference to her former life as a grade school teacher. "I'm going to need lots of help."

Sarah didn't remind her that they didn't know how secure her future was at the moment. After all, Hillard had changed Sarah without the permission of the Vampire Council – the punishment for which was normally death for both the creator and created one. She had been trying not to think about that being the possible reason for Hillard's absence. She didn't even know if her attempt to keep her thoughts blocked off from the Vampire Council was working or not. However, that direction of thought led only to more worry and unproductive speculation, so Sarah pushed it forcibly to the back of her mind.

"So, what *do* you want to do?" Sarah asked, curious. She assumed that Christine must have had something in mind when she came into the room.

Christine looked conspiratorially at Sarah. "Let's explore this place," she said. "No one's here. Giselle's at home with her husband and Gervis is with his parents. There aren't even any guards!" Christine very obviously skipped over the fact that the reason that there were no guards was that Lord Radek had slaughtered them all the day before. "We have the whole place to ourselves!" she exclaimed gleefully.

Sarah had to admit that her curiosity was peaked. Having been born and raised in Thunder Bay, Ontario, she had never seen a real castle before this one, except for in pictures and on TV. This was a real opportunity. She grabbed Christine's hand and practically dragged her out the door.

Several hours later, the girls had almost finished exploring the enormous castle. They had walked through kilometres of stone hallways, peeked into numerous extravagantly decorated bedrooms, and had even trekked up a long circular stairway into a tower room. It was dusty and filled with wooden boxes and discarded junk. It was obviously just a storage room, but Sarah was charmed by the round shape of the room and the gorgeous view from the window. From that vantage point, they could see an identical tower on the other side of the castle. Curious, the girls dashed back down the stairs and through the castle, wanting to see what treasures the other room would hold.

When they opened the door to the room, however, both girls just stopped in their tracks with shock. This space was starkly different from the other. There was no window in this room, and no junk or boxes littered the floor. There was even a neatly made bed sitting to one side, indicating that someone slept here, at least occasionally. What had the two girls paralyzed with astonishment, however, was the room's lone occupant.

Sarah doubted that the poor child (she assumed that's what it was because of its size) had ever slept in that bed, though. Placed as far away from the bed as was possible in the tiny room, was a cage. It was approximately two meters square, with thick iron bars and a thin, moth-eaten blanket lining the bottom. The child cowered in the corner of the cage, her stringy brown hair scraggled and knotted around her head. Sarah had never seen a creature so pathetic in all her life.

The young girl stared intently through the bars at Sarah and Christine, making small mewling sounds in the back of her throat. Despite the lack of a window, the room was cold and Sarah wondered how the child didn't freeze to death, given her nakedness.

She was just starting to wonder how on earth this child had come to be in this room, when the truth hit her like a brick wall. This was another one of Lord Radek's atrocities. She wondered if he slept in this room and kept the child around for a 'midnight snack' or if he just sadistically enjoyed inflicting such horrendous suffering on such a small innocent victim.

After a moment of stunned silence that seemed to last an eternity, both women stepped forward.

"My God, Sarah," whispered Christine in horror, "She's practically a baby! What was he *doing* with her?"

"Nothing good," replied Sarah, grimly. She knelt on the floor in front of the cage, trying to bring herself to eye-level with the child.

And what beautiful eyes she had! A stark contrast to her dirty face, her green eyes shone out of the filth. Although not the same glowing emerald green as either Sarah or Christine's eyes, they had a delicate beauty of their own and seemed to hold a keen intelligence within.

"What's your name, sweetie?" asked Christine, kneeling down beside Sarah. The girl just stared at the two women silently. Her gaze was slowly changing from one of fear to a more measured curiosity. She remained still.

Sarah got up and began searching throughout the room for a key to unlock the girl's prison. It took her only a few moments. She found it easily enough under the pillow on the bed – there weren't too many places to look in a room containing nothing but a bed and a small child in a cage. She tore the blanket off of the bed and tossed it to Christine. "She must be freezing," she said by way of explanation, then strode back to the cage. It took her a moment to unlock the door – the lock seemed to be rusty and unused. The hinges creaked as the door swung open, granting freedom to its pathetic captive.

The girl paused for only a moment before dashing out of the cage and across the room, flinging herself under the bed. Sarah thought that she was hiding under there, afraid of the two women, until she heard the girl make a grunting noise and an answering squeak-squeal sound. The girl shimmied back out from under the bed, and then sat  back up on the floor holding her prize, a large rat, in front of her.

Sarah's first, naïve, thought was that the rat was the girl's pet, something she watched running around the room, perhaps even playing with during her captivity. That thought was coldly proven wrong when the child raised the rat to her mouth and abruptly bit off its head. She spat the head back towards the cage and then began to suck greedily on the open wound that was oozing blood.

Horrified, Sarah and Christine both just stepped back and stared at the appalling sight.  The child didn't appear to be a vampire. Her eyes did not have the unnatural emerald sheen that thus far had indicated someone with the vampiric nature.  But, if she wasn't a vampire, what was she?  And what had Lord Radek been doing with her?